To Trust in What We Cannot See

Dennis Mansfield

TO TRUST IN WHAT WE CANNOT SEE

iUniverse books may be ordered through booksellers or by contacting:

iUniverse
1663 Liberty Drive
Bloomington, IN 47403
www.iuniverse.com
844-349-9409

Because of the dynamic nature of the internet, any web addresses or links contained in this book may have changed since publication and may no longer be valid. The views expressed in this work are solely those of the author and do not necessarily reflect the views of the publisher, and the publisher hereby disclaims any responsibility for them.

Any people depicted in stock imagery provided by Getty Images are models, and such images are being used for illustrative purposes only. Certain stock imagery © Getty Images.

Cover Design: Guy/Rome, guyrome.com
Cover Illustration: Robert S. Harrah

ISBN: 978-1-5320-8325-9 (sc)
ISBN: 978-1-5320-8324-2 (hc)
ISBN: 978-1-5320-8326-6 (e)

Library of Congress Control Number: 2019916236

Print information available on the last page.

iUniverse rev. date: 04/29/2024

Prologue
January 1913

The hallway smelled of stale cigarette smoke and something rancid, something I didn't really want to identify. I slowly walked to the door of the young artist. The man, Adolf Hitler, was loosely known among some denizens of the art world as a painter with only modest talent. He was twenty-four years old at the time.

History records indicated that Adolf Hitler saw himself as an architectural artist, forced into making a living painting silly postcards and selling them to locals and tourists. Not yet involved in politics, he desired to be accepted in time to the famed Academy of Fine Arts Vienna. That never happened.

I knocked on his door. Silence.

Then, slowly, the door opened, and standing eerily before us was young Adolf Hitler.

"Guten Tag. What may I do for you?" he said.

Dr. Russ Gersema and I stood speechless.

Not knowing what to say, I simply asked, "May we come in? We'd like to see your art."

He paused, looked us over, then nodded and opened the door.

"I hope you have plenty of money with you," the future killer of six million Jews said with an awkward and unbusinesslike tone.

As he closed the door, Adolf Hitler turned back to both of us and then peered strangely at my covisitor; it forced my attention toward him too.

My partner in dimensional spacetime travel, Dr. Russell Gersema, held a Steyr-Mannlicher M1912 semiautomatic handgun pointed directly at the forehead of the father of the future Nazi movement.

And he pulled the trigger.

1

Present Day

Literary critics say that every good story needs a villain, so I suppose this might just turn out to be a great story because it has historical men of immense villainy.

It's the story of the twentieth-century murderers who destroyed nations, killing groups of people and eliminating generations—a small group of criminals who killed millions of men, women, and children from 1917 to 1945.

Imagine if when these maniacal, middle-aged men were younger, that by happenstance or providence, you or I could do something to change *or even end* their lives, at one time and in one place. What would the world be like today?

What if the fabric of time and space allowed us to do it … and on another level fought against us while we changed history? What if we could see the many worlds that came into being due to the absence of these tyrants and choose which world we'd like to live in?

That is this story.

While I'm not a widely read author, I didn't choose to tell this story; it chose me. I've authored nonfiction books and coauthored a few fiction books, yet none has so captivated me as has this tale.

I couldn't even *think up* this story as a fiction piece if I had wanted to, nor could I have lived it. But I think I did live it.

And I wasn't alone.

I met Russ Gersema in a coffee shop in Vienna.

It wasn't a Starbucks …

Vienna doesn't like Starbucks.

Europe either, I've observed.

The funny thing is I don't even like coffee.

However, visiting coffee shops for long hours in Europe *does* have its benefits for even a coffee bean celibate like me. Some of it is the vibe; some of it is the lovely roasted coffee fragrance. For me, it's fairly simple: when I'm traveling, I don't have an office, and I need a place to think and write. Coffee shops work for this—and for parking a bike and meeting friends.

I'm a biking enthusiast. Over time, I've biked in some amazing cities. I enjoyed trekking across Iceland's capital city, Reykjavík, as well as Germany's capital city of Berlin and down the Danube, across the Austrian farmlands. I've biked Paris and stood next to where Victor Hugo lived and where Jim Morrison died, hoping, I suppose, for some deep inspiration to accost me.

Generally, I find bits of inspiration parking my road bike, sitting outside of a beer hall or inside a café, watching people, jotting down notes—experiencing strangers' lives from a safe distance. Watching people allows me to witness human nature as it unfolds, one story at a time, without any disruptive and inconvenient chance of actually entering into their lives. It is virtual life lived out in real life—comfortable and distant. Each city or town offers a particular café or pub in which to sit, watch, and push a pencil, strike a keyboard, or jot notes on an iPhone.

Another personal benefit of European coffee shops is being able to increase my European weight. The daily thick lattes and sugary coffee drinks offer *that* as a possibility for all who visit. *Ah,* but as I said, my tastes don't go to java, so the truer danger lurks elsewhere—in a brimming, hot cup of dark, almost black, liquid chocolate, the scent of which hovers at cafés' doorsteps each morning, inviting all willing victims to enter and grow fat.

Not American fat, just European fat. There's a difference.

Each morning in Vienna, I park my road bicycle at Herrengasse 14. Café Central greets bikers, pedestrians, tourists, and locals. The smell of hot chocolate draws me in, once again, like a lover obsessed. This particular morning was a rough ride. I took a spill right outside of the café, protected by my bike helmet but missing an Austrian driver by just inches as I rolled to the side of the small street. The smell of chocolate came at me as I lay on the ground, cajoling me to stand and enter Café Central, which I obediently did.

Since 1876, Café Central has been seducing and healing many. She's an aged adulteress. I can't run from her. I can't even bike from her. I simply surrender, paralyzed, like those before me.

It's been my recent life's work to replace each early-morning's biking episode (and supposed weight loss) with the zero-sum gain of hot chocolate shots and pastries. I comfort myself with the failed thinking that, for a century and a half, people have eaten at Café Central in Vienna and died; no amount of weight loss and biking will preserve a happy life. Eat, bike, and die.

Chocolate, on the other hand, lives on; it soothes all ills and allows slight moments of happiness to live forever, even as generations come and go.

I stood with a smile at the counter near the entrance, in front of a man I would soon come to know. I didn't know it then, but he would change my life forever.

I ordered my morning fix of piping-hot "Viennese Chocolate." It's so seductive it stops all conversations before they begin. At that moment, there's only one thought, only one love.

Well, there might be a second: Austrian pastries and cakes.

Over the years at the famed Café Central in Vienna, pastries, cakes, and crème-filled confectionaries have been served to hungry customers—enjoyed by a cross section of men and women, one pastry at a time, one bite at a time, the customers reluctant to finish such incredible food.

Often, for historically short periods, customers become prisoners of their own appetites, each renting history just for today as they eat and sip. Today, I am a prisoner in the current generation, occupying one of many booths around the outside edges of Café Central, enjoying pastries and hot beverages. Maybe it's not as current a generation as one would think, since pastry prisoners often hear older songs by groups like the Beatles as background music. The listeners age, yet the music's themes stay put.

My personal pastry favorite, the crème-filled Patisserie Chocolate Cake, was how this man came into my life. It's more accurate to say that a final *remaining* crème-filled Patisserie Chocolate Cake forced us together.

I ordered the rich, deep dark chocolate cake with its traditional crème-filled strawberries and then heard a deflated sigh behind me. A Midwestern accent seemed almost detectable in the comment spoken under his breath (but only to another American, I suppose). Next, he approached the clerk and placed his order, sans the desired heavenly, delicate cake. He then hung back a bit from the people at the counter, a misplaced, hungry American sitting alone with his thoughts.

"Welcome to Vienna," I said as I handed him my trophy dessert. "I believe this is yours?"

He looked surprised.

"No, actually, the man in front of me ordered that. I wish it were mine," he said with a slight smile.

"Well, I am that man who was in front of you, and this patisserie has your signature on it as a guest." I paused. "I'm here regularly anyway," I said as I extended the plate to him. "I'll have mine tomorrow."

He laughed the sort of light chuckle that had more to it than my comment required and then replied, "That's very kind of you. My *signature*, huh?"

"Yep. American, right? Midwest?"

"Almost. Kansas City. You?"

"Pacific Northwest," I replied.

He delicately manipulated his fork, unsheathing a portion of the cake's perfect top pastry layer. Once in his mouth, his eyelids reverently closed shut, as if in prayer.

I understood and sat quietly sipping my chocolaty morning shot-cup, silent in the reverence.

"May I join you?" I then asked.

"Of course, of course," he mumbled as he was licking his lips.

"What brings you to Vienna, my fellow American?" I asked.

He set down his pastry plate, picked up his small cup of Viennese coffee, and took an extended sip, as though either regaining his composure from this taste of heaven or preparing to measure his words for other reasons. I wasn't sure.

"Nineteen thirteen."

I paused. "Excuse me?"

"Nineteen thirteen brings me here. Directly here."

I wasn't sure how to take this odd response. I cocked my head and said, "Well, I think you're a little late."

He laughed. "Maybe not."

He looked up at me from his cream-filled vacation break. "Umm, do you know what happened here in 1913?" he asked as he pointed a couple of times to the ground with his fork, slowly licking the frosting from his lips when he finished the question.

He had a genuine way of speaking—a kind way, as if he was fully present and wanted me to learn.

I stumbled a bit with a few ums and ahs, finally recovering with a quick (and, I thought, pithy) response. "As an author and historian, I'd say elegant Vienna was at the terrible threshold of this continent's first European war—"

"No. I mean right *here.*" He stabbed the fork into the air above the café's floor, while at the same time moving his other hand in increasing semicircles. "At Café Central. Right where we're seated."

I was dumbfounded, looking at him as though the international travel guru, Rick Steves, was quizzing me about a tourist spot.

"I have no idea."

This tall, early-forties Midwesterner reached his hand toward me and said, "Oh, please excuse me; that's very rude of me to just launch in with such a strange response to your honest question without even giving you my name. Let's start with that first. Okay?"

I nodded and took his hand. "I'm Russ Gersema, from Kansas City, Missouri," he said.

I returned his handshake, introduced myself, and responded to the typical question strangers tend to ask one another, "What do you do for a living?" I told him I was an author of seven books, with an eighth on the way.

"Eight books? That's wonderful. *Wonderful.* What genre?"

"Actually two genres—historical fiction and biographical nonfiction. My first book came out about five years ago." I saw him glancing at the traces of gray and silver in my hair.

As if apologizing, I said, "I became an author later in life."

He paused and took a long look at me. "Eight books in five years—that's a fast pace." He paused again for a few seconds. "Author, not *writer,* I noticed you call yourself."

"I'm not a writer. I don't put together prose for others—clients or ad copy. I write from my own authority, hence the title of author."

"Explain that."

"Well, I was married for many years. I lost my bride ten years ago. A publishing company approached me a few years after that to write about what I had endured through that experience."

I paused to put in check my unexpected emotions.

He responded, "I'm sorry for bringing up such deep pain."

"No, it's … okay," I said, rather unconvincingly. "You asked about *author* versus *writer*. My pain, as you put it, actually pushed me forward. I wrote the book about pain, and it's been published, forcing a type of authority on me that I would never have chosen. Since that point, I've authored other books."

He nibbled some more, all the while watching me, watching my eyes.

"We have something in common," he said, quickly adding in embarrassment, "I mean, I mean we have something professionally in common."

"You're an author too?"

"No, but I do appreciate authors *and* writers—especially those over the years who write from their personal experiences, as you do." He looked at me. "I'm genuinely sorry for your loss."

I thanked him for his kindness and understanding. The unintentional and awkward pain made its exit.

He savored another bite of the chocolate cake, cleaning the silver fork with his thin lips, which were barely visible under his full moustache. I remember thinking how his face resembled that of a man from the turn of the nineteenth century.

Then he laughed that type of hearty chuckle often reserved for only close friends. "Author? Me? No, I'm not an author. I dabble a little in science, and I am a collector and seller of books, rare books." With an arched eyebrow, he quietly added, "Very rare signed books …"

"Really? How rare?"

"Oh, I don't know. Nineteenth-century rare, some in the early twentieth century."

"Good for you," I said, realizing that it sounded as though I was patting a child on the head. "I mean, it sounds difficult."

He smiled his chocolaty grin and let the matter lie.

Searching for common ground, I said, "I collect books too. My office is full of 'em. Maybe more accurately it's that I collect autographs that just happen to be inside books. Certainly not rare autographs or rare books."

He looked hard at me and with intensity stated, "All autographed books are rare. Each book touched the hands of the person whose story is in that book."

He paused. "Do you get that?"

I responded, "I suppose I do."

He took another sip of coffee.

"Do you sign your books?" he asked.

"Sure, when someone asks me to do so. Some are autobiographical books about history, touching on *my* history, I suppose, and the history around me. Even my fiction books flow from personal experiences of mine or others I know. I experienced the events of the books I write, so, as I said, I have the authority to pen them."

Leaning across the small table with clasped hands and deftly moving his cup aside with his elbows, he asked, "Do you have one of your books in your backpack?"

Embarrassed, I wondered how he guessed I might have one on me.

"Come, come, *Author*, no need to blush when a paying customer asks to buy a book! Get it out and show me. I'd like to own one of your stories."

I reached into my backpack and withdrew a dog-eared copy of my third book, a fiction tale of a young man on a wild adventure. "I have this copy ..." I said with a slight pause.

My new friend opened his wallet and placed a twenty-euro banknote on the table. "This should cover it, don't you think?"

"No, no, no. Please allow me to give it to you as a gift." I found my voice raising, but I didn't know why.

"I tell you what. I'll take your free copy of—what's the title?"

"*A Change of Time*," I answered.

"Okay, a free copy of that one, if you'll allow two requests," he said. I nodded in agreement.

"First that *I* can pay for the cakes and coffee tomorrow——"

I interrupted with "And hot chocolate?" We both laughed.

"And second, that you autograph this copy right now."

Again, I nodded yes.

"Great. Write this: 'To my new friend, Russ Gersema, on our delightful time at Café Central in January 1913."

"What?" I said with a twist of my head toward him as I reached for a pen.

He smiled. "Those exact words or no deal."

I opened the flyleaf and wrote exactly as he said, writing slowly so that I didn't smudge the gel ink.

"So, you're famous? Penning autobiographies would make that seem so," he said nonchalantly.

"No, not famous at all," I replied as I finished my inscription and placed the Café Central promotional pen back on the table. Embarrassed by his questioning, I glanced at the floor and then looked up at him, apprehensive that this new acquaintance might ask me how many copies each of my titles have sold.

He picked up the book and the pen and glanced past my inscription as he placed a thumb on my signature and pressed down, briefly closing his eyes, whispering a word or a number as he did so. I couldn't tell. Putting both the pen and the book into his sport coat pocket, he turned and looked at me.

I felt a sudden chill run down my spine—the kind we all experience in winter when an open door lets in the cold. Summer doesn't often lend itself to that sensation.

He said, "You know, in a real way, all history is simply a collection of written anecdotal experiences, isn't it? Many authors remain unknown. Most are undervalued." His decision not to query me, as some strangers do, about the tonnage of books sold seemed intentional and even kind.

He paused and then continued, "Each book I collect has its author's autograph sealing the personal nature of history— various authors drawing together their readers, helping each of us to better understand ourselves through their lives. When they sign their books, their physical DNA touches all that came from their minds. It's really quite amazing."

He looked out past the busy Austrian waiters and flow of customers, seemingly over the din of the plates and cups, almost as if none of those things were even there.

I was slowly warming to this soft-spoken, pensive man.

I interrupted the momentary quiet with a question. "So … 1913? It's obvious I'm not as well versed an historian as I've pretended to be."

"Oh, no, again, please forgive me. It's a bit complicated, and I certainly don't wish you to feel slighted by my comments. Would you allow me to rephrase my response by asking you a question instead, *Author*?"

"Certainly." Then with a smile, I stated, "And please don't call me that. My first name will do."

He looked at me, smiled, and ate some more of his (and my) treasure, gently holding up the café's beautiful silver fork as a delicate tool, as though it were a baton and he a conductor.

My enigmatic new acquaintance wiped a small amount of crumbs from his moustache with a lace napkin, the color of edelweiss, and leaned over to me as we sat at the table near the front. He asked me one simple question.

"What do Lenin, Trotsky, Stalin, Hitler, and Tito all have in common … *other* than the obvious?"

He interrupted himself. "Allow me to throw in Emperor Franz Joseph, Archduke Franz Ferdinand, and Sigmund Freud, for good measure."

Rick Steves was no longer quizzing me. International historian Stephen Ambrose took his place.

"I, I … ugh—"

He cut me off—I think to save my fragile and failing sense of self-worth.

"They were all here in this very café in January 1913."

I looked at him bewildered. "What? Together?"

His twinkling eyes seemed to shout. "They were around each other regularly in this elegant Viennese coffee shop! They were here, and the world never knew it, nor could they have known it."

I was shocked. I asked him to repeat what he had just said.

"They were in this café, day in and day out—enjoying the cakes and coffees we both enjoyed today. One hundred-plus years ago, these men sat near each other reading newspapers; playing chess with friends; discussing the politics of the Austro-Hungarian Empire, England, Germany, and the Balkans—nations just ready to explode into regional conflict and, in time, to cause a world war—actually, to cause two world wars.

"In fact, it's often been repeated by locals at the Café Central that young Stalin played a game of chess with young Hitler." He paused. "No one knows who won. Ha!"

My alt-history teacher continued, "We *do* know that young Trotsky played chess with any and everybody here. It was also here that Lenin eventually met with Trotsky. In time, Lenin made the introduction for Stalin to come to Vienna and meet Trotsky for the first time in late January 1913—*right here.*"

I blurted out, "Imagine if something accidentally happened, at just *that* moment—or any other of the moments—that could have changed the course of the European wars!"

He stared at me and said, "Yes. Think of that."

Lost in this new moment, I added, "Think of what could be done if we could go back in time and see them together, here in this place ... and do something."

"Yes," he muttered under his breath, "and *do* something."

I caught his change of tone, though not the meaning. I shivered again, unsure of whether it was the cold or his tone that had again gotten to me.

He paused, collected his thoughts, and then smiled widely, stretching out his arms in the way a man does when he wakes up in the morning. Then he took his final sip of coffee and said,

"Indeed, *Author*. And that's just the start of it." He rose from the table, drawing me to my feet, as well.

I stared at him, a bit bothered by his reuse of this new nickname and more than a bit stunned by the history he was telling me; it was a minor personal irritation mixed with huge global fascination. On this very floor space, in this deliciously decorated Victorian-era café where we'd been sitting, once sat young men who would change the entire world. The lights seemed to flicker a bit. For some reason, I hadn't noticed that the café's lights were gas lit.

Russ Gersema looked at me, taking what appeared to be his final visual inventory of "the author" and then nodded toward the door. Strange, I could hear horse hoofs on the street. I looked out our window to where I had locked my bike, helmet, and gloves to the bike stand. They were *all* gone.

He looked at me, stroked his moustache, and said, "Shall we take a stroll?"

2

1913

As we exited the café, I don't know what shocked me more—the sheer cold air or the smell.

The odor of sewage nearly overcame me. The temperature dropped to what must have been thirty degrees Fahrenheit, buckling my knees.

Off to my left side—where my bike had been locked—was a crew of wooly-clothed workmen holding either pickaxes or shovels, most leaning against a horse cart, all smoking pipes and looking down into a large pothole, the center of which held a broken clay pipe. Sewage was seeping out of it. What struck me was how none of them seemed to be in a hurry. Nor did the smell seem to overwhelm them, as it did me.

I spoke to them in my broken German. "Wissen Sie wo mein bike ist?" They completely ignored me, looking at one another and then staring into the sewage hole they were digging.

"Don't worry. I know when your bike is," my walking friend said to me.

I stopped. "Don't you mean *where*?"

"Yes, I do, *and* I mean when."

Snowflakes were coming down. I looked up.

Everything around me had changed. Horses and carts, carriages and pedestrians were everywhere. Cobblestones echoed the clanging sound of horseshoes plodding along.

In an instant, as I felt the cobblestones under my soles, I also felt the weight of the clothes I was wearing. They were made out of harsh and heavy wool. And someone else's hat was snuggly on my head.

It was extraordinary. I felt like a man unsure of whether he was waking up from a dream or entering into one.

I looked into the same *platz* through which less than half an hour ago I had ridden my bike on a sunny summer morning, and saw nothing familiar. *Nothing.* Men in suits made of thick fabric with overcoats hanging loosely on them walked side by side with women in long, flowing dresses, holding winter snow umbrellas that seemed to collide at times with their large-brimmed hats. They all seemed to be strolling—none in a hurry.

My new friend, cavalier about the change, yet obviously seeing my confusion, turned to me. "Quite amazing, isn't it?"

I screamed, "What just happened? Where are we? *When* are we?"

We were both dressed in ill-fitting suits, nothing like we had worn inside the café. These were thick wool suits with long weather coats over them, coming to our knees, purely functional for keeping us from the surrounding cold weather.

I stood still. "How? What? I mean ... wha-what?"

Turning to face me directly, he spoke in a near whisper. "We are travelers. I'll explain when we get to my flat. Right now, all you need to know is that we are still in Vienna, though the month is different—along with the year."

"The year has changed? You *live* here?" I sputtered.

"Yes, the year has changed—obviously the month too. And you might say I've been coming to Café Central a lot longer than have you. It's now 1913. Remember?" he said with a slight smile.

I must have looked shell-shocked, for clearly I was stunned. "Remember what?" I managed to squeak out.

"Remember when I asked you about January 1913 back at Café Central?" he said as he motioned over his shoulder with his thumb toward where we had just been.

"Yes."

"This is what I was referring to. This is Vienna in January 1913."

As we walked, he said, "Author, do you believe in dimensional travel?"

I shook my head back and forth slightly. "You mean time travel?"

"Well, not really. *Dimensional* travel. Interested?"

"I've lost you. What are you asking me?"

We turned a corner and kept walking.

"I'm asking you, as a creative person, if you really could insert yourself into dimensions, tucked within history, and change things, would you?" He didn't seem to want me to answer.

I couldn't answer; I had become a sleepwalker as he talked.

As we kept walking, he directed me to the right, up a slight stairway of three blueish stained steps. He stood in front of me and unlocked the large oak front door. We entered his flat, and he motioned for me to place my thick outer garments on the hallway coat tree as he excused himself to another room. I obeyed.

I stood alone in the hallway for a few minutes, looking at whatever seemed interesting. I noticed artwork, carpets, a skinny couch with only one side of it that supported an armrest. I couldn't help but notice the loud, colorful wallpaper in the hallway and ascending the staircase as well. I had seen many of these things over the years in black-and-white photographs of the Victorian age. Yet, here they were in living color and relatively new.

"Oh, you noticed the fainting couch, did you?" he said as he emerged from the room. He left open the door and walked toward this strange piece of furniture. "Apparently, it's all the rage in America and Europe—allowing people prone to regularly swooning with a place to land as they enter their host's house."

He paused and then burst out in laughter. "Feel free to make use of it; you deserve a good swoon right about now!" I suppose his laughter brought me out of my ambling half coma. I shook my head no, even managing a smile myself.

"Whatever has happened to us, my guess is that I may really need that couch later," I replied.

He laughed again, an easy laugh. Then he invited me into the room from which he had come—his library.

It wasn't the kind of library I would have expected though. Certainly there was the sliding wall-to-ceiling ladder to aid the reader as he or she searched for books near the top shelves. I anticipated looking up to see rows of leather-bound books. Instead, on the walls of his library were maps—a dozen or so very large maps that reached from floor to ceiling. Around them, on the edges, were much smaller maps, temporarily attached—it seemed—by irregular clumps of melted candle wax.

He saw me focusing on the wax, especially as my eyes followed the candle drippings to the floor. "Sorry for the candle wax. Tape hasn't been invented yet." Again, he laughed. "It won't be until 1930, when 3M's Richard Drew develops it. And I haven't gone shopping for it in time for our meeting today."

I squinted my eyes and shook my head from side to side, not knowing what he meant.

My host sat down in a comfortable-looking chair and motioned for me to join him in the adjacent sofa chair. Next to it was a small, stand-alone half bookshelf that held a small assortment of books.

"Well, would you?" he again asked.

I looked at him, confused, still shaking off the fuzziness. "Would I what?"

"Would you return to Café Central and change history by doing something drastic to one or all of those people I spoke to you about?"

I paused, taking the fuller measure of Mr. Gersema.

"I suppose I would, if it were possible. Wouldn't you?"

He gave me a wry smile and answered in a clipped voice, "Yes."

I finally flinched, realizing that somehow we were actually where Hitler lived and the others had their flats. They worked nearby and enjoyed coffee and cake together at Café Central. The past was now present, and we could do something. We could do anything we wanted.

And apparently my host was planning on doing something. I wasn't quite sure.

Gersema said, "Before we touch what's happening, please allow me to do two things. First, if you would, allow me to give you the background on how this works."

I nodded forcefully. "Yes, that would help me greatly."

He continued, "And second, you might be wondering why I selected you to join me on this encounter with time and space."

Quiet suddenly separated us.

I looked at him, wondering what he meant by the use of the word *selected*.

"You selected me?"

He nodded.

It never occurred to me to consider what I thought was just a chance meeting. Stating it as he had just done stopped me cold.

More time passed.

I said, "Yes, then, that would help. Let's cover the second issue first, shall we?" Sarcasm dripped off each word.

Russ Gersema smiled and then laughed a bold, full-throated laugh—one that most of us use when something catches us by surprise.

I looked at him again, even more confused.

He wiped the tears from his eyes with his handkerchief. "Author, please forgive me for my response, but I've grown over the past year to appreciate your sense of humor and irony, and today you didn't let me down."

"This past year?" I asked. "We just met this morning, Mr. Gersema."

"Oh sorry, I slipped," he responded, putting away the handkerchief in his top, left suit coat pocket.

"You what?" I replied quickly.

"I slipped," he said in measured tones. He quickly added, "Maybe this will help. Let's set aside that second issue and logically tackle the first issue: traveling in time. It may well clear up a few of your initial concerns: How does this work? How did we make our way to Vienna in 1913 through time and space? I promise that it will also answer your concerns about us meeting. Sit back and listen, if you will."

I settled back in my large sofa chair, hoping that he just might be able to assuage my concerns about having been selected and him apparently knowing me for a year or so.

"All right. Proceed," I said.

He crossed his legs, adjusted the crease of his pants, dusted off a piece of lint from them, and looked up at me. "Have you ever read your copy of *The Elegant Universe* by Brian Greene?"

I stopped, a bit stunned. "Actually, I do have an autographed copy of it. How did you know? A friend gave it to me years ago when it was first published. I never got around to reading all of it."

"You should have. It's a national best seller, originally published in the last year of the twentieth century. Dr. Greene was a Pulitzer Prize finalist. He received his undergraduate degree from Harvard and his doctorate from Oxford, where he was a Rhodes scholar. Professor Greene changed the thought process of many, many people about spacetime through his book."

I cupped my chin in my hand as I leaned into the armchair and replied, "I suppose you're right; I probably should have read it, but I failed calculus in college." I sounded far too apologetic. As if to patch the emotional hole, I added, "Which then allowed me to concentrate on English, ultimately leading to my current career. Physics doesn't seem to be something I particularly charge into easily. I was too busy reading and writing while listening to James Taylor in college for inspiration, let alone years later, to fully read my friend's *math book* gift. "It sounded so defensive, so petty."

As if ignoring what he could clearly see in me, he laughed. "You're not alone. I *did* enjoy reading and writing, but my focus was math and science. I read works by Newton, Einstein, and many papers on the subject of relativity. I also enjoyed James Taylor … and the Beatles.

"*The Elegant Universe* finished for me the process of examining what we call time and space—by seeing things differently. Seeing things for the way they are and not for the way I've always experienced or learned they should be."

"How do you mean?"

"Well, to begin with, when I say, 'Isaac Newton,' you respond with what?"

"Cherry tree."

My new science teacher shook his head, "No, that's George Washington." He chortled. "C'mon. Help me here."

I laughed too. "Okay, let's go for apple tree for $200."

"Ding, ding, ding. Yes, you are correct. And …"

"And … Isaac Newton invented … gravity," I hesitantly answered.

"My God, Author, I've read your writings; you are smarter than this!" he said with mystery in his voice and a laugh.

"You've actually read my works? What?"

"We'll get to that in a bit, as I said, but for right now, let's get some things straight. Isaac Newton *discovered* gravity; he didn't invent it or create it. He discovered it, though he didn't actually know what it was, which led to an incredible series of other discoveries and writings, of experiments and global influences that Isaac Newton accomplished. For example, three hundred years later, Albert Einstein considered Isaac Newton to be the most brilliant man who ever lived. Much of Einstein's work found its base in Isaac Newton's thoughts. Dr. Greene expanded on much of what Einstein was searching for."

And then my science teacher and historian added, as if to connect the dots, "You might remember, even James Taylor penned 'Einstein said that we'd never understand it all.' Does that ring a bell?"

I nodded; I could hear the song in my mind and smiled.

"Brian Greene changed my thinking. Allow me to explain," Gersema said, not allowing this dramatic moment to pass. "Einstein's theories of special relativity and general relativity amended Newton's groundbreaking work, changing much of what we know today to be true. Or better yet, *truer.* He did not just build on Newton's work; he remodeled it."

I scrunched my eyes together, committing all my mental faculties in the direction of my science teacher. "And that brings us to Dr. Greene's book how?"

"I'm glad you asked that *and* that you stopped singing the James Taylor song in your subconscious."

I just looked at him. *How does he know these things?*

"How many dimensions are there?" he suddenly asked in a tone reminiscent of an older sibling asking a younger one what their home address is.

"Four," I said confidently. "Everyone knows there are four dimensions: height, width, depth, and time." Apparently even my F grades in college math still allowed something to stick all these years later.

"Just like everyone knew and believed that Isaac Newton had the final word?" he asked.

Ugh, I thought, *an F in math again.*

I paused, recovered, then added, "Okay, Dr. Greene Fanboy, tell me where we're going with this in our $E = mc^2$ time today."

Gersema simply responded, "Eleven."

A long and awkward pause ensued, reminiscent of the conversation in Café Central regarding the year 1913. My breathing increased. I spun my body toward him.

"You are freaking me out. What does eleven even mean? What is happening here?"

"Eleven dimensions. *The Elegant Universe* and Greene's subsequent work make the case that there are eleven dimensions that surround us in nature. Dr. Greene's work is magnificent and groundbreaking. It's changing the twenty-first century—allowing you and me to change the late nineteenth and early twentieth centuries."

"Explain what these eleven dimensions are," I said.

"Okay, listen up," my coffee shop physics teacher said. "Brian Greene put it this way: these ideas emanate from Albert Einstein's desire to develop a unifying theory—that everything in physics is connected and works together and that someone can *and will* find the theory that unifies it all.

"There appear to be ten dimensions plus time, hence the eleven." He paused and took a sip of water. "Within the ten dimensions, it may be that we've been unable to perceive them, possibly because they're too small. Another alternative theory is that light—which is how we perceive the first three dimensions, length, width, and depth—may not travel to those dimensions, which are spatial dimensions, not temporal ones."

He smiled and then simply stated, "In my research, I have now disproved the alternative theory regarding the use of light in those other dimensions."

"Which means what?" I asked as I leaned toward him.

"Which means, dear Author, that we can now harness the light, shine it into those other spacetime dimensions, and travel to see what is there. Realize, though, that fundamentally the dimensions are the same stuff as the three dimensions that we're familiar with; they just have different shapes and sizes. They can be extremely small."

I regained my composure and asked, "As in quantum mechanics small?"

He nodded.

I added, "And in the past, the lack of light was the key differentiating element that kept us from seeing these other dimensions?"

"Exactly," he stated with a smile. "And so I have added to Dr. Greene's work, as he did to Einstein's and Einstein did to Newton's. You and I are standing on Dr. Greene's shoulders, as he did on the shoulders of the others, peering into a new world where theory finds its actualization in motion through light."

"What do you mean?"

"What I mean, dear Author, is that I have found the method by which we can actually travel between and among these eleven dimensions by harnessing light—by directing it into the other dimensions. Entering into worlds that parallel ours, we can, if we choose to, change those worlds, see how life would be lived if things were different … if people and things were different. And then select *that* dimension for the world to be where we live."

"By 'if things were different,' you mean if people were dead—people like Hitler, Stalin, Trotsky, and Tito?"

"Don't forget Sigmund Freud," he answered. "And no, not necessarily dead. I said *different*."

"Okay, different. How so?"

"Well, before we get into the specifics, shall we now tackle the second question: how did I select you?"

I studied him as he looked at the full, glass brandy decanter on top of the small bookcase to my side. He walked over to it, picked up the decanter, and poured into a small brandy glass. "You're gonna need more than hot chocolate once you hear the story."

3

1913

After sipping from his glass of brandy, he spoke slowly. "Here's a riddle. Your books aren't particularly why I sought you out, yet your books are exactly why I sought you out."

I looked at him and cocked my head. "All right, Riddler, does that mean you don't care about my topics, but—"

He interrupted. "Oh, I care about what you've written. Having read every one of your books, I enjoy your style, though at times your content is a bit too vulnerable for my tastes. But then again, I don't share much about … my lives."

I winced at how he brought up having read my books, and I winced even more at his choice of the word "lives." *Eight books read in one day. Nah. Not buying it.*

He continued, "It was through your vulnerability that I actually was able to do an incredible amount of homework on you."

"And that's another thing. Where do you come off saying that you've read all my books? We met only this morning. I never met you before that," I said.

"If a person takes the time, anything is possible. Good students find out what their subjects like and don't like," he answered, tipping his brandy glass in my direction, as if in a toast.

I picked up my tumbler.

"I am a student of you. Here's to things you hate!" He toasted with his tumbler toward mine.

I took a sip and shuddered, thinking, *Why am I drinking brandy? I hate this stuff.* He smiled.

"Like brandy?" he said with a laugh. "I served you a tumbler of it, knowing that you'd actually hate the stuff."

"Really?" I said as I self-consciously set the glass and its contents on an oriental woven coaster atop the small bookshelf. This was getting odd; I began to feel quite uncomfortable.

"So, you've been stalking me because you *kind of* like the books I have written, yet those books are not the reason why you've been stalking me—in Vienna, in the winter, in 1913? Do I have this all correct?" I asked, my voice nearly trembling.

He nodded. "Except this: when you said, 'books I have written,' you could have said it differently by saying 'my books.' Why did you choose your words so precisely?"

"Well, because there are many books I own that are under the category of 'my books,' although not books I've authored."

I paused, looked off to the side, then repeated his words, "Your books aren't particularly why I sought you out, yet your books are exactly why I sought you out.

"Ah. You're not talking about the books I've authored; you care about the books I own."

He smiled. "Well done, Batman," he said and then polished off the remnant of the tumbler he'd previously been nursing.

"You own a select assortment of older books, of which a few hold very special significance to what I face at Café Central. Or I should say that *you and I* face at the café."

"I'm lost," I said. "How does the owning of books mean anything, and how did they move us back through time?"

"You mean through spacetime."

"Whatever."

He moved past me and set his empty tumbler next to my glass. Returning to his chair, he asked, "Does the name Orrin Backus mean anything to you?" Russ Gersema shifted in his chair, just as he was shifting in our now fascinating discussion.

"No. Should it?"

"Well, allow me to put that name in context. Orrin Backus served in the United States Civil War on behalf of the Union Army as captain in charge of the steamer *Diadem* from 1861 to 1865. He transported troops, food, and munitions—first running these supplies past Rebel attackers on the tributaries of the Mississippi and Ohio Rivers. He later took part in many military excursions and expeditions with Union General A. J. Smith's Sixteenth and Seventeenth Army Corps. He was a part of a Colonel Gilbert's Iowa Twenty-Seventh Regiment on the Tennessee River, the Yazoo River, and the Red River. He helped transport tens of thousands of Union soldiers across all these rivers to attack the Confederate Armies during many battles."

"Fascinating," I muttered as I sat wondering where he was going with this.

He knowingly looked at me just as he reached over for my tumbler of the god-awful brandy and continued, "Backus worked for the United States government but was not a member of the armed forces. He was a businessman and riverboat pilot."

"Okay ..."

He continued, "So that gave him the unique perspective of meeting many Union generals as they used his river transport services to either escape *or* attack—depending on the nature of how strong the Confederate forces were—and where they were located.

"Now bear with me for a second. I'll connect the dots in a way that will surprise you, just as I was taken off guard."

"I'm waiting ..."

"One of the generals was Ulysses S. Grant," he said, as though suddenly it all made sense—or that it should.

It didn't.

I looked at him as he stood with his arms open wide, as though he had just unveiled the ah-ha of all time.

I asked sarcastically, "Did we miss a drumroll?"

For the first time, I saw him really frustrated. His eyes bore down on me. "Okay, let me put it to you this way. In the latter part of the twentieth century, you received a gift purchased at Josef's Bookstore in Riverside, California. The gift was a two-volume set titled *Personal Memoirs of Ulysses S. Grant*."

I gulped, remembering the anniversary gift from my wife when we were young. I wondered how he knew something that was mine to so easily forget.

He continued, "It was an 1885 first edition, autographed copy of former United States president Grant's last written words—his memoir, prepared and published by Mark Twain as the general was succumbing to throat cancer." Russ didn't need to ask if he was correct or even if I had read it. My face showed he was accurate.

"What in the world does all this mean? Yes, I own that rare set. Yes, it was a gift. And yes, I read it!" I exploded.

Gersema settled back into his chair, clipping off the end of a cigar he had extracted from a wooden box. He lit it, puffed a bit to get it started, and then took a long drag from it. As he exhaled, all I could see through the volume of blue smoke was his Cheshire smile.

"And whose name was penciled in at the top of the first volume?"

We both paused, him egging me on with the slight up and down movement of his head and eyes, as if to say, "Remember."

"Orrin Backus?" I asked, feeling that this circle of questions had to have an end and he was drawing us to just such a point.

Then I said, as if only to myself, "He was the original owner of my book."

He slowly blew another ring of cigar smoke toward the ceiling. "Well, yes, of the book you *later* owned. Apparently there were only two families that owned it. His and yours."

My rare-book-stalking, hard-drinking, laughter-filled new friend began to open wide the story of how the original owner of the book changed the face of Southern California after the dissolution of hostilities between North and South in 1865.

"You see, after the war, Mr. Backus returned both to his native Ohio and to the business partnership with his brother, Lafayette, where they once again engaged in what was then called the mercantile business of groceries, clothes, and other miscellaneous items. Columbus was the hub of their business concerns."

I couldn't help myself; I leaned in closer and listened, genuinely interested in the life of the man who, twenty years after the end of the Civil War, purchased the newly printed, autographed copy of former president Grant's memoir. The Backus brothers: Orrin had a brother named Lafayette.

What an exotic name for a plain Ohio brother, I thought.

"You've done your homework, Mr. Gersema," I said.

He ignored me and continued. "Ohio eventually gave way to California, when Orrin Backus's first wife died." He paused, realizing what he had so matter-of-factly said to me. His eyes seemed to apologize, and then he continued. "He left all he had and started over, moving to Riverside City—at that time a part of the county of San Bernardino, California. Along the way, the record on his brother, Lafayette, appears to stop. The only other mention of him is when he died in 1914.

"Orrin Backus and his son, William, formed W. H. Backus in Riverside, growing orange orchards and vineyards, developing the citrus and raisin industries and making money. Ultimately, they found banks, businesses, and real estate holdings, allowing people to comfortably and easily relocate from the frigid east to the far more temperate climates of Southern California."

The fact that I had owned Grant's memoirs for almost four decades—originally owned by an eyewitness to Grant's role in the Civil War—and had not known it was remarkable to me.

"This is interesting certainly, yet I can't help believe that there's more to all these facts and Backus family history lessons. Right?" I asked, honestly wanting to piece together the scraps of what any historian would call unimportant local events.

My new friend answered, "There is."

He continued. "It's taken me what most people would call years to get to this point in my discovery process. I've been like a cat with eleven lives ..."

I nonchalantly corrected him. "You mean nine lives." I brushed off lint from my rough wool slacks.

I looked up, measuring the sudden silence in the room.

"No, I mean eleven lives," he said as seriously as if he was responding to an insult. "Just like the dimensions."

"Okay, sorry for the erroneous idiomatic expression." I checked my new friend out. It seemed that he didn't care much for my sarcasm.

Gersema had been searching for several years to find a first edition, autographed copy of the former president's memoirs, and he was intent on communicating to me the immense importance of this puzzle.

"Look, Author, here's the deal," he began with absolutely no hint of humor in his voice. "Yours is the last existing copy of that autobiography—the only one with the signature of Orrin Backus in it. You've got it hidden away somewhere. And together you and I can use it to help change history in ways too large for either of us to fully comprehend as we sit here in the twenty-first century."

"You mean the twentieth century." I then corrected myself: "Or I mean twenty-first century." I did not want to get further blasted by him.

He looked at me, his brow relaxed, and he did what he hadn't done for most of this conversation: he laughed.

"Do you know what ley lines are?" he said. "They involve energy and time. YouTube is full of wild people who talk about this subject."

I smiled and said, "My guess is somewhere in this jumble of 1913, 1865, and 1885, I'm about to find out."

"Oh, yeah, you'll find out. But let's return to the café, and I'll show you how we traveled from this morning to last century."

He nodded toward the coat rack.

For an author committed to having the authority to write what he has experienced, I was becoming an experienced hostage to history.

I looked at my host/captor, who quietly asked, as he swirled his final sip of my brandy, "How about another cup of hot chocolate rather than this fine product?"

I rose to my feet and joined him in a smile as we headed out of the library and toward the front door. "And a pastry?"

We both smiled. His was real.

As we walked the relatively short distance to Café Central, Dr. Russell Gersema chatted away about Vienna in 1913. I listened and took visual inventory of this man.

Short, scholarly, yet erect as he walked, he had a way about himself that combined his eyes and jawline into an intense sort of investigative look. He was a man on a mission, and I somehow seemed to be a part of it, though I didn't quite know how just yet.

We must have been a sight, he with his short strides, his blond hair, cut short, his animated arms and hands as he talked. And me with my long strides born out of miles of bike riding, my longish silver-gray hair, and my willingness to follow his lead, though I had no idea where we were going ... until my nose gave me a hint.

We turned the corner to our left, immediately smelled the bakery, and entered the lobby. Café Central welcomed us once again.

After several hours of sitting in Café Central, listening to Russ Gersema, I was *alive*.

I'd asked him questions while sipping many cups of cocoa, eating not enough Austrian pasties. We sat in the booth—close to where we'd met decades ago in the future (or was it just hours ago in the past?), and I began to understand the topics he'd just shared.

Time held no boundaries to our discussion. I'd never had this happen in my life; my mind and body were at peak attention.

"Well, Author, repeat back to me the key principles that I've shared with you today. You talk now, and I'll eat. I am famished!" He shoved a huge portion of cake into his mouth.

"That's, uh, a tall order, but I'll try," I replied.

He immediately interrupted through a mouthful of cake, "Dere is no trwi-ing." He gulped down the large portion of cake that had just crossed over the threshold of his lips. He quickly cleared his throat. "There is only doing." He forced the next big piece of the cake into his mouth. His behavior was quite animated.

I replied, "I'm not sure whether to thank Yoda or Elmer Fudd, but yes, I'll do it and skip the trying." I paused. "So, a man named Watkins, Alfred Watkins … right?"

He nodded his approval, looking at his plate.

"Watkins was an early-twentieth-century shop owner whose family milling business demanded that he travel by horseback through rural towns in England. He was also an amateur photographer who took his large camera with him and, when time allowed, snapped images of the English countryside. So far, so good?"

Again, my calorie-dismissive friend nodded.

"And in taking landscape pictures, he noticed some strange things. For example, as he set up shots, he saw that many of the familiar places and landmarks were in absolute straight lines—expanding out for miles and miles. These included lines connecting churches, holy sites, wells, burial areas, chambers of significance, mounds made by people, roads made in ancient Roman times, and even stone circles." I paused. "A frustrated artist trapped in a shopkeeper's apron, it looks like to me."

Gersema said nothing but moved his fork like a maestro's baton in a couple of small circles, signifying that I continue.

"Maybe it's better to say Mr. Watkins was an amateur archeologist stuck behind a frustrating photographer's tripod. Either way, he kept snapping away, looking for ancient sites all over the English countryside."

Gersema motioned to our café waiter, pointing first at his now-empty plate and coffee cup and then upward with his right thumb and index finger as he ordered. "Zwei, bitte," he said, then turned back to me, making direct eye contact. "Wie heissen Sie?"

"What?"

The waiter interrupted. "My name is Gunther." He had a young girl next to him. "And this is my daughter, Frieda."

"Danke. Thank you," Gersema said.

Still looking at me, Gunther asked, "And?"

I couldn't help myself. "Hello, my name is Author," I said with a smirk and then looked at the little girl. "Frieda, why are you here with your father at work today?"

The little Austrian girl, about nine or ten years old, smiled and said, "To watch my Papa and learn how to do what he does."

I patted her on the head, reached into my pocket, and flipped her the only coin I had, an American quarter. "Always remember what the American word *tips* means!"

As the coin turned in the air, I said, "To insure prompt service!"

She smiled as she grabbed the coin midair and stuffed it in her skirt pocket. "Danke."

"Bitte," I responded as she and her father walked away.

Doc's eyes went half-dead, with slightly upturned corners of his lips signaling me to continue.

I went on, thinking myself ever so clever. "So, Watkins ended up coining the term *ley line* to signify observed lines on the maps that connect all these sites. I suppose he wanted to get the *ley of the land*?"

Gersema just stared at me. I could tell that my cleverness might best be used on another day for a less focused moment—or at least until his angry-hungry appetite was satiated.

His fully dead eyes told me to continue. The slight smile evaporated.

"And in the early 1920s, he wrote three books. The most noteworthy was something—I think—called *The Old Straight Track*." I paused. "Did I get it right?" I hated that I sounded like a student looking for a good grade. But I suppose I was.

My ley line instructor nodded his approval to the waiter as the next round of Café Central's delicacies were delivered to our table. He looked at me. "What?"

"Did I get Watkins's book title right?"

He answered, "Principles, Author. Principles! I want you to understand the main thing, so whether you get the title right or not is of no concern to me at this point."

Gersema's fun-loving nature was absent, replaced by the intensity brought about, apparently, by his foray into what I could only understand as a conflict between hunger and the pseudoscience/voodoo science of ley lines—a world in conflict with his true scientific worldview.

I repeated to him what he had previously taught me, how Watkins felt that there was some type of earth energy field found in those straight lines that resonates with our personal energy needs, as if they were survey lines with electromagnetic power attached and felt by each one of us.

I finished up with how Watkins spent the last years of his life putting together his theories, trying to find out why these lines had this electromagnetic attachment to them. It was a fruitless dozen-plus years; he never succeeded.

Gersema finished the last bite of his second piece of cake and dabbed the corners of his mouth with the beautifully edelweiss-colored linen, making sure that he cleaned the space between his lip and the large nineteenth-century moustache of his.

His color returned, as did the life in his eyes. "Well done."

I shyly smiled in response.

He continued as he looked at the person to whom he had just spoken those words. "Well done, Gunther."

I felt embarrassed.

He looked at me, laughed, and said, "Well done to you too, Author. You nailed it."

I laughed as well. "Man, without food, you are one hangry guy!"

"Without Viennese cake and coffee, I am."

We both leaned back from the booth's table and rested against the comfortable, cushiony backs, holding lightly with our half-filled cups.

"Let's start by defining terms," he said. "Ley lines is an unacceptable expression for me; it's an entry ticket into the really weird world of pseudoscience and wannabe archeology. I refuse to use that word."

I looked at him—confused he had even used the term.

He seemed to understand my confusion. "I wanted *you* to hear the term, so I used it as I explained the broad principles of the tasks into which we are currently heading. No offense to the armies on the internet, fans who meld science and New Age theories into their various beliefs about these straight-arrow lines, but as a PhD, my fields of study in electrical engineering and physics demand that I live in the world of pure science."

"Wait, you're a doctor?" I asked. "Like … an inventor? A discoverer? Like Newton?" I smirked a bit too widely.

He looked at me and nodded.

"Others can choose spiritualism, emotional vibes, Hinduism, Christianity … I've never found the need for that sort of thinking. No offense to your faith, Author."

It was my time to smile. "None taken. I live in the world of facts as well, so I understand."

He looked at me and cocked his head oddly. "Hmm. Well, when it comes to these electromagnetic lines, I prefer the term *telluric currents*. It captures the underground nature of an Earth in birth pangs of sorts. Hot streams of water, earthquakes, volcanoes, and energy release all bring the hard edge of science to those willing to study them," he said.

I was struck by something he said. "So, instead of thinking about the soft underbelly of embracing UFOlogists and conspiracy theories, you prefer to treat time travel as fact? I'm a little confused."

He looked around the café, as I'd witnessed in my past among these secretive types, as if to see if any future famous faces had arrived. None had.

He continued. "It's dimension travel, and you be the judge, Author. You're currently seated in a café in Vienna in the winter of 1913. It looks real to me *and* scientifically observable—even repeatable—once you learn more from me."

"I suppose you're right, *Doctor*—er, I mean *Doc.*"

He seemed a little irritated at receiving a new name; it was my time to turn the blade and then to laugh.

Without missing a beat, he asked the question I'd been wanting to know since we moved through time and space: "Would you like me to explain how I use telluric currents to move us from one dimension to another?"

I smiled, which must have said it all.

"Well, let's head back to my library, and I'll unveil my DeLorean to you, future boy."

He caught me off guard, and then I chuckled, realizing his reference to *Back to the Future*.

He added, "We'll travel at very fast speeds, so be prepared." I flinched a bit, then nodded as we exited the café's door.

"How fast?" I questioned as we took the now-familiar turn toward his flat.

"Well, let's just say it's faster than eighty-eight miles per hour," he responded, shooting a side glance to me.

4

1913

Much of my earlier visit to Russ Gersema's flat was spent in a state of mind that I can only refer to as *spaceship jet lag,* if there could be such a thing. During the last visit, I couldn't believe I was *where* I was; nor could I accept the date. This time, it was somewhat different, though still strange. I accepted it; I just didn't yet understand it.

While walking the cobblestone streets, I caught glimpses of people who should have been dead a century earlier. Yet there they were, smiling, hugging their spouses, and strolling in the winter snow on a *platz* of a city even lovelier than when I had ridden my bike over it a hundred-plus minutes ago ... or a hundred-plus years from now.

The smells, the sounds, the feel of fabrics and strange hats all combined to make me understand what sleepwalkers feel seconds before they're abruptly awakened.

I was about to ask my new friend, *Dr.* Russell Gersema, what to expect as we turned the corner toward his small, Victorian-era, first-floor flat. However, I decided to pause.

"You don't really mind if I call you Doctor, do you? After all, Author's not quite my name."

He looked at me blank faced and then simply nodded once as we kept walking.

"Okay, Doctor, when we were at your place earlier, you had maps all over the walls of your library. How do you use maps in planning to use ley lines?"

"Telluric currents."

"I mean telluric currents; that's a bit of a mouthful. How about if we just refer to them as TCs?"

"Shorthand terms are acceptable," he said in a monotone as we trudged in the cold winter weather of Austria, frost blowing from our noses and mouths as we spoke in measured sentences. "TCs it'll be."

I exhaled and saw even larger clouds of frosted air leave my lips as we walked together at a quick pace, born out of necessity. "How can we map travel via the TCs?"

He continued in the same gait. "Well, let's start with something simple to best understand how we'll do it. For example, you and I would have no trouble mapping the equator, would we?"

"No, not at all. Nice weather there, by the way." I paused. "Umm, your travel plans wouldn't involve, say, an immediate warm visit to Ecuador, would they?"

"Not today." He finally chuckled. "We'd draw the line around the center of the earth, knowing that such a straight line would connect all points, with no deviation: one line, one point. Right?"

We turned the corner and kept walking.

"Yes."

"And we'd have no problem mapping latitude and longitude lines, labeling each according to their accepted numbers, correct?"

"Correct, though we might need to ensure that the numbers we assign them are accurate and match the standard, global numbering system."

"Very true, Author; sounds like you're remembering some of your physics and geography undergraduate studies."

"Yeah, just don't bring up calculus, okay?" I chortled as I said it, shivering even more from the memory than from the current cold.

He continued, "Well, TCs have a similar structure and accuracy to them, just at different angles. They circle the globe, as do the other lines we've just mentioned, though it's very interesting to see just how accurately they connect key cities—even key centers within the cities—allowing for energy to pass through those connected areas. It remains that way year after year."

"Century after century?"

"Yes, Author." Then he added, "Dimension after dimension."

I heard it but didn't quite grasp it. I wondered, *Where are we going with this?*

The street became familiar once again. We were at his flat, ascending the small stoop of steps. I noticed three small steps dripping in a blue liquid; the ice had melted only on his blue stoop.

"Who would have thought that Austrians would have this ice-melt stuff a hundred years ago?" I exclaimed, surprised.

"They don't; Walmart does. One of the nice things of dimensional travel. Next shopping trip, I'll grab the Post-it Notes and tape."

I laughed as we strode up the steps.

Passing through the front door and past the unneeded fainting couch in the hallway, discarding coats and scarves onto the coat tree as we walked toward the doctor's library, he blurted out, "Let's take a look at the first map on the wall: England. What do you see, Author?"

I studied the flat map of England; lines crisscrossed the island, seemingly in random patterns. I stood searching for some pattern or intricate design.

"You're giving it too much of your attention," he said. "Look at it; describe the lines!"

I inched closer to them, staring at how they jumped across the United Kingdom from one town to another, one portion of the land to another with only one characteristic: they were straight.

I responded, "Well, they're straight lines; they go from off the island onto the beach toward a town, through that town, over hills and mountains to other towns and cities, and then finally off the island and across the channel, toward other land masses."

"Exactly." He smiled. "Now, look at the map off to your right, over past the bookcase ladder—the one of the United States." I moved as he asked me to.

"Do you see anything unusual on that map?"

I couldn't help but see the obvious. "Yeah, there's a thick, straight line that passes along the eastern seaboard attaching Boston, New York City, and Washington, DC." I paused. I'd never before thought about how absolutely straight and in line these cities were.

"Indeed," he said. Pointing to other lines that crossed this line and headed west, he said, "Do you see those other lines heading toward the Pacific Northwest in North America?"

I leaned in, looked, and then nodded.

He redirected me to another large wall map directly behind us and over near the large fireplace. "Take a look at that map," he said as he pointed to the colored map of Europe.

Across the very large map was a two-colored X. The long red-colored line originated in the UK and came diagonally across from northwest to southeast, from the top left to the bottom right. The thick green line was opposite it, originating in Madrid, Spain, at the bottom left of the map and going straight to the top right, directly into the center of Moscow, Russia.

"Now, take a closer look at Madrid," he directed. I obliged. "Do you see the line coming from America's Pacific Northwest, perpendicularly intersecting the line connecting the eastern seaboard from DC to Boston?" I nodded. He continued, "Follow that new line across the Atlantic Ocean. Where does it go?" he asked, knowing all too well the answer.

I saw the geometry. It went directly through the center of Madrid.

I simply looked up at him with what must have been a strange, searching look on my face.

"I'm not done yet, Author. Search out the cities along the third straight line from Madrid to Moscow; what city is included within that straight shot?"

I followed the line with my finger and then stopped, unable to go any farther.

"Vienna," I said.

"Now scoot over to the expanded version of the Vienna city streets map—the one attached to what you were just examining." I moved a few inches over to see this very intricate city-sweep map with streets and avenues everywhere, crisscrossing just as you would see for any city in any country, with one exception: a large red line cutting straight across the city.

He continued, "Look for where the red line cuts directly through the city."

I stared at the map, seeing the red line cut through open spaces, a large city square or platz, and intersect only two buildings: one at Herrengasse 14 and the other just a short distance behind it— the very house in which we were now standing.

I stood up and looked across the room at Dr. Russell Gersema, my eyes the size of small German-chocolate cake plates.

"This flat is one of the two buildings?"

"Yep," he responded with deep satisfaction. "And the other?"

I bent back over the map and followed the streets, retracing the roads in my mind until the obvious answer emerged: Café Central.

I shot up. "Oh my God."

He nodded, reached for that bottle of brandy again, poured two more tumblers, and handed one to me.

This time I took it and drank it down without even pausing. He reached into his pocket and pulled out the autographed copy of my book, *A Change of Time,* he'd asked me to sign back in the café earlier that morning.

He pointed to the title and coyly remarked, "Get ready. Your title says it all. I've got to send you back. I just hope you're not too late. He may already have gotten there."

"Who?" I asked.

"Lafayette Backus," he responded.

"What are you talking about? Where?" I said, flustered and caught off balance.

"Where Hemingway died, dear Author, where Hemingway died."

5

Present Day

I love to travel, yet home is always Boise, Idaho—not a big city, in not a big state, yet a great airport and easy connections. Living is nice in Idaho.

It's an interesting and historic area of America in which I work and live. In the first decade of the 1800s, Lewis and Clark's Corps of Discovery did just that. They discovered what would one day be known as Idaho; next they traveled through the area that would be called Washington.

Sacagawea, their intrepid Indian guide, gave birth to a child, Pomp, on the trip, who would later rise to European fame, speaking five languages, impacting many. Ultimately, he would return to Oregon, where he would die and be buried in the land his mother helped discover.

The Pacific Northwest is almost always spoken of in the following cadence: Washington, Oregon, and Idaho. The first two obviously are next to the Pacific Ocean, but all three have seaports. *Really.* Idaho's seaport is in Lewiston, with oceangoing vessels docking there, traveling the mighty rivers of that region— delivering and picking up goods on the rivers that Lewis, Clark,

Sacagawea, and her babe in arms traveled when Thomas Jefferson was president.

Meriwether Lewis, William Clark, and Sacagawea found the Pacific Ocean through Washington, Oregon, and Idaho. So, I suppose it's the name of the ocean that provides the ticket for admission to the Pacific Northwest club.

Clark's fate continued long after Lewis's untimely death. Ultimately, his family tree sprouted branches that spread and overshadowed the hot and arid land of California. My own family sprang from this family tree. My lifelong fascination with travel (and the history of the two voyagers' journey) is this generation's fruit from that family tree.

I moved to Boise, Idaho, a long time ago, fleeing San Bernardino and Riverside in Southern California. I don't think we even looked in the rearview mirror as we climbed our way out of Southern Cal's Cajon Pass.

Idaho was our destination. I suppose it had always been my destination. The adventures of my family that called me home to Idaho.

My upstairs home office overlooks the often-raging Boise River. Memories and mementos grace the walls, showing a family with many adventures: vacations and trips to Iceland, Europe, and Israel. They're photos of a life fully lived, I suppose.

The office walls are also packed with bookshelves. Wave after wave of classic works pound down on my thoughts, as though they're hoping for my own future classics to come to life and join them. (Not happening so far.) My book sales are typical for authors and writers in America—not as many as any of us want them to be.

The Boise River rushes at uncomfortable water flow rates, released by unknown municipal assailants in far-upriver dams. I experience the river as a crew coxswain that yells at me through an unpowered megaphone: "Write faster! Dig deeper!" While I *row* in this office-hull, history, science, and long-ago lives float past me.

I live (and crew) in the past, writing in the present, for stories of the future about places I have seen and those I would like to visit one day. Ah, but it's the past that grabs hold of me, book after book, shelf after shelf. Seeing the signatures of the authors reminds me that they too sat for weeks, writing, editing, writing, reediting. Their autographs bring me back to the authority of their books; they lived it as they wrote. In some cases, they relived it as they wrote.

I enjoy collecting books—not for investment, unless one considers investing in one's own knowledge as something of noncommercial value. Like others, I enjoy well-grounded, well-researched books on history. Collecting books with signatures seems to make the stories come alive even more for me.

World Wars I and II (along with books on the Cold War) occupy large spans on my shelves, books ranging from one of Churchill's many works, *The Gathering Storm*, to the single work by the highest-ranking Communist official ever to defect to the West, Romuald Spasowski's *The Liberation of One*. Autographs are everywhere.

Spasowski's inscription to my wife and me reads, "To my new friends, with thanks for your help and prayers, May 14, 1986."

Churchill's book, *The Gathering Storm*, has his signature on the flyleaf page. Nixon's book, *Six Crises*, is inscribed, "To my good friend from President Nixon." I guess I was Richard Nixon's friend too. Churchill died before I could be his good friend, I suppose.

Nothing pre-WWII by Ernest Hemingway though. Some authors' works are too rare.

Sitting in Boise, just two hours away from where Hemingway lived and died, I can't help but wish I could see what he saw, visit where he visited, write as he wrote; but then again, he used up four wives and one liver doing what he did by the time he was my age. I might reconsider.

It's so odd to think I am the same age as Hemingway was when he blew his brains all over the rotating ceiling fan in Ketchum, Idaho. He came back to Idaho to die. I came to Idaho to live. I got the better end of the deal, I think.

Hemingway's Europe holds sway on my mind, even as it's changed since his time there. I love biking in Europe. Especially through those countries that straddle the Danube. Austria grabs my heart, and Vienna, my soul.

Science fascinates me as well. Sometimes the two interests overlap in all their subsets—military, technology, science, history, and physics, each with slightly connected edges.

I travel to write. I also read as I go places, hoping that as I read and write, I can channel that travel for others—maybe shut-ins, people who need faith and hope, those who read Hemingway and live, not people who want to die like Hemingway.

For example, Sarah Dry's incredible autographed work, *The Newton Papers*, sits on my desk and details the remarkable prewar discovery and subsequent auction in 1936 of Sir Isaac Newton's almost universally unknown manuscripts on theology and alchemy. In a scientific community largely resting on the shoulders of Isaac Newton, this breakout discovery of Newton's relatively unknown writings forced even an agnostic Einstein to consider how he subsequently must experience a religious version of his mentor.

Near that book on my desk stands *The Elegant Universe* by Professor Brian Greene. It's the book Dr. Gersema loves. To say that the book is earthshaking is to limit truth to our small solar system. Science and physics, dimensions and travel—all these aspects combine together in his book, I'm told.

Then there are the European war books.

The prewar smiling faces found in black-and-white photos in many of my books about Adolf Hitler's rise to power contrast starkly with his own clearly evil words found in *Mein Kampf* and the little-known additional book he wrote in 1928 that was later published in the 1950s, titled *Hitler's Second Book*, which I also own. The author signed neither of these books. The army officer who found the second manuscript in a Nazi file after WWII signed it instead. There are no smiles in this section of the bookshelf, only blame and hatred. They rest on my shelf, seething.

So, how was it that the Nazis embraced such evil?

Maybe it was one amended custom at a time, like something as small as changing how one salutes military leaders. Kaiser Wilhelm II favored the typical right-hand salute to the brim of a hat or helmet.

Hitler changed that.

Many books show readers a time when millions of Germans, Austrians, and conquered civilian peoples joined their military Nazi victors by raising their right arms with outstretched hands lifted stiffly upward in a common international gesture of respect, at the time called the Roman salute. Hitler didn't develop the salute; he used it to unite large sections of the world with it. Italians had used it for years with Mussolini's increasing stranglehold of power.

American civilians saluted that way as well.

From the early 1890s to the 1940s, the custom of all American citizens was to stand at attention and repeat the Pledge of Allegiance with their right arms outstretched and lifted up diagonally at Old Glory, in what was then called the Bellamy salute. Photos in books of pre-WWII America present this strange sight, though current American history books are selective in what they show.

In some military books, there are Americans holding their arms in the same salute, including Charles Lindbergh. Shocking at first, some history books help the reader through the awkward dilemma. Many don't. Just as in no longer naming new babies "Adolf," the Roman salute had a short shelf life once WWII began.

It took a few months after Pearl Harbor—even with Hitler declaring war on America—for the US Congress to change the flag salute to placing one's right hand over the heart, as we now know it.

So it stands that not everything we do today is what they did in the recent past.

The evil of Hitler changed everyday life, even for a harmless, morning American flag salute by elementary school innocents.

In the harsh clarity of history's rearview mirror, it's almost impossible to think that there once was a time when people were close friends with Adolf Hitler. Even he was a little boy, an adolescent, and a young man with hopes for his future.

These were likely not the hopes of a megalomaniac, seducing crowds, standing in rapt attention, rigid with Nazi salutes. Rather, they were the hopes of a young man for friends—personal intimates with whom Adolf could sit and have a meal or a beer and stretch out on a sofa and talk about life, friends who shared in lighthearted conversational banter about the day's events. This type of storyline for Hitler's young adult life escapes both Nazi hunters and Nazi apologists.

His level of demonic evil doesn't permit historians to afford him any such retroactive humanity.

However, history as a force can ignore historians, forcing them to learn unfiltered facts. Archeology—history's natural first cousin—teaches that one only has to dig for those facts.

In post-WWII, it's almost impossible to find books about Hitler's personal life, unless the authors are psychologists or military historians.

Almost.

As one who writes daily, I also read daily—with a goal of many books each year. Doing so sharpens my writing ability. Stephen King, in his nonfiction masterpiece, *On Writing*, unknowingly became my tutor. He says that he reads immense amounts of books each year; therefore, I do too. He's fascinated by time travel and dimensional changes, as am I. We all tend to learn from those we follow.

I hunt for books with unusual backgrounds written by interesting people about whom I initially often know very little. The hunt leads me in many directions and toward many *very* different authors.

So, it was when I received a surprising addition to my bookshelves—a published first edition copy of *Hitler: The Missing Years* by Ernst "Putzi" Hanfstaengl—that my life took a decidedly different turn. Written on the first page in barely legible left-handed cursive is this:

Christmas 1948

Dear Smith—This may seem a rather odd gift, but I thought you might be interested in the fact that I spent an evening with the author—Putzi Hanfstaengl—a friend of Beatrice Schubert's— and hence was briefly, as it were, just a step removed from the nefarious Hitler. How time passes! Love, Louise

I consumed the book. The author's vivid description of the young man Hitler drew me again and again to the question, How did this young person become the most nefarious international monster for this century and all centuries to come?

The book offers story after story of a young would-be artist from Vienna whose life seemed destined for ignominy and anonymity. Yet, reading it seemed like watching a terrible event unfold—an imminent car crash or a man jumping to his death yet still on the ledge. I didn't want the book to end, yet due to Hitler's poisonous words and actions, I couldn't wait till it was finished.

Upon its completion, I was drawn again to its inscription. Something seemed odd.

I couldn't quite put my finger on it.

I thought it would be good to meet Louise and ask her about this author, Ernst Franz Sedgwick Hanfstaengl, who was known to his friends (including Adolf Hitler) as "Putzi." Also, I'd like to know who Beatrice Schubert was—a name that she and Smith so obviously knew.

Better yet, it would be good to meet Putzi and talk with him—about Hitler and the dinners, beers, and talks with Hitler.

Or even to meet Hitler.

It's not unusual to find personal inscriptions on the fly pages of books—something written as gifts given in commemoration of one's birthday, an anniversary, or, in Louise's case, to "Smith" as a Christmas gift. I've learned over the years of reading autobiographies that when a book has both the autograph of the author and some type of other personal inscription, the book becomes a double mentor to me, besting even Stephen King.

Still, something has bothered me about Louise's inscription, and I can't quite figure it out.

On my bookshelf in Idaho, next to Putzi Hanfstaengl's book has always been the autobiography in which the good doctor expressed such keen interest—written and autographed by an American author who was born sixty-seven years *before* Hitler and seventy-seven years before Hemingway—of a former US president who was utterly broke and dying of cancer at the time Charles L. Webster and Company published his book, rocketing it to immense international success.

Ulysses Simpson Grant.

Charles L. Webster and Company published Grant's autobiography in 1885, just weeks before cancer accomplished what no lone rifleman or any large army could during the Civil War.

His signature rests on the first page of this first edition, two-volume set of his one and only book, sitting on my desk 120 miles away from Hemingway's desk.

It also has that additional autograph of Orrin Backus. Like the Louise of the future, Orrin left his penciled thoughts from the past throughout the book as an eyewitness to many of General Grant's actions during the War of Rebellion, as both men referred to it.

Other than just being on my bookshelf, a very odd bridge connects Putzi Hanfstaengl to U. S. Grant. One man: Union Army General John Sedgwick was known to his troops as "Uncle John" and was a friend so great to Grant in May 1864 that when Sedgwick was shot and killed by a Confederate sniper, General Grant hung his head and repeatedly asked in complete despair to no one in particular, "Is he dead? Is he really dead?"

Putzi Hanfstaengl's mother was an American citizen, and his father a German. His grandmother as well was a well-connected woman—all friends of Mark Twain, *they say,* and the first cousin and friend of US Army General John Sedgwick. She was so deeply hurt by the death of her cousin—the highest-ranking Union Army officer to die in battle—that twenty years later, she named her son Ernst Franz *Sedgwick* Hanfstaengl, after the Union Army general.

Putzi was raised both in the United States and Imperial Germany. He was as comfortable with Imperial Court ministers as he was with American elite.

As a graduate of Harvard, he was well connected in both the American and German governments from his college days on, and he counted Theodore Roosevelt and Franklin Roosevelt as friends.

To a nobody like Hitler, Putzi seemed to have the keys to the future, and he used those keys to open doors to this often-unkept Austrian friend who regularly slept on his couch.

In his book, *Hitler: The Missing Years,* Hanfstaengl described the then-young Adolf Hitler as one who "looked like a suburban hairdresser on his day off." I laughed out loud when I read the wonderfully awkward and colorful description of a man who in just a decade would be seen only as a colorless, demented killer.

Yet someone from WWII, named Louise, liked the book enough to give it to Smith for Christmas in 1948.

Nineteen forty-eight?

That's it. That's what didn't make sense to me. That's what I told the good doctor about.

It's why, back in the 1913 version of Vienna, he had me place my hand on my own signature of *A Change of Time,* and I stepped onto the TC that ran through his office building, hurling me back to the office in which I wrote the book, sending me back to Idaho.

I went to my desk bookshelf, quickly turned to the title page, and read the name of the English publisher—Eyre & Spottiswoode, London—and then I saw what I was searching for: the publishing date.

Nineteen fifty-seven. What?

I searched every page, turning them like a madman, looking for pencil markings by Louise—the type I'd seen marked up by Orrin Backus in his personal copy of Grant's memoirs. I was searching for anything that would explain this to me.

"Explain what?" I said out loud. "That a person named Louise gave a man named Smith a book for Christmas nine years before it was published?"

Her faint pencil markings were not out of the ordinary for the type of person who reads and at the same time jots down notes on that page. There were many comments, some about *this* politician and *that* dinner party. All very normal. Nothing not normal, except the dates.

As I made my way upstairs, I reached into my pocket and pulled out the note in the good doctor's handwriting:

1. Get the autographed book by Putzi on Hitler as well as Hitler's second book.
2. Grab the signed Grant volume.
3. Bring *The Newton Papers* book by Dry.

4. Do *not* forget the signed copy of Dr. Brian Green's *The Elegant Universe.*
5. Grab your iPhone.

—Doc

P.S. Bring back your copy of *Grays Sports Almanac.*

I laughed. Check, check, check, and uh … no! Doc apparently did indeed have a sense of humor, I thought as I stuffed the needed goods into my additional Rick Steves backpack. I left the previous one I had back in Europe. *Why not this one too? No one here needs it,* I thought. *This house hasn't seen visitors in quite a long time—or has it?*

That thought made me stop. I picked up my iPhone from the table and checked my video security app.

The time code showed a visitor had been in my home, in this very office. The camera picked up an extremely clear image of him.

For the most part, he kept his back to the camera. Then, at some point, he slowly turned around toward the camera and looked directly into the lens. His eyebrows were furrowed; a kind of keenness mingled with malevolent intensity seemed to emanate from his face. He didn't appear to be just some common thief. He had a sense about him that could easily be understood as a man of power and force—a man on his own mission. I studied his face, his mocking smile. He turned and was gone.

I looked around my office and my desk to see what he could have taken but did not see anything missing. Out of instinct, I captured his image on my iPhone and then sent it to my HP printer for a paper copy. Folding the paper, I placed it in my back pocket.

I looked over at my writing desk at another image—a school photograph of my wife's fifth-grade class, taken as they saluted the flag for her class picture. Taken the autumn before her passing that next spring. So many tender faces, led by my wife of so many tender years.

"I love you. I wish you were still here," I whispered to her image.

I headed down the stairs to the front yard, opening up the copy of *A Change of Time* while putting my thumb on my own autograph. I stepped out onto the telluric current line and closed my eyes.

In an instant, I slipped the bonds of this dimension and was gone.

1913

Something happened to us earlier that same morning in 1913 at Café Central before I left and returned to the present in Idaho. It portended to be significant, especially for Doc. We met Miss Lou Abraham.

She was seated across from us. She had caught the eye of Dr. Russell Gersema. Apparently, the interest was mutual. She motioned to the waiter. He had a little girl next to him. I could overhear her comments, though they were softly spoken. Her accent gave her away—American.

"Gunther, would you mind doing me a favor?" she asked, nodding to the little girl next to him.

"Why of course, Fraulein Lou. What do you wish of me?"

Lou scribbled down a brief note on the back of a visiting card.

"Would you mind taking this note to that table where the two Americans are eating, seated near your waiter's station?"

"Certainly." He took the note and departed, with his young daughter, Frieda, trailing behind him.

As Gunther and Frieda delivered the cursive note to us, this woman turned and looked at us. Doc read the brief note and smiled broadly.

We waved to her. She returned our waves. We motioned for her to join us at the much more spacious booth we occupied. This young postgraduate student made her way to our booth. We stood and greeted her.

"Good morning, miss. It's always an honor and privilege to meet another American traveling abroad in Europe. Allow me to introduce myself. I'm Dr. Russell Gersema." He extended his hand, and she politely shook it.

I followed in the only way I was becoming accustomed to around Doc. "I'm Dr. Gersema's student, Arthur ..."

She glanced at me but focused on Doc. "Oh, so you *too* use postgraduate students."

He nodded and said, "Uh, yes. You could say that. Your note on the back of the card caught our attention."

"Oh yes, it's a translated expression in English that my uncle Max gave me years ago. My German is *schlect*, but his Jewish humor always seemed to bridge language."

"I'd say." I laughed as I picked up the card and again read it. "Your family is Jewish?" I asked as a natural follow-up in what I thought was a normal voice.

"With my last name? Of course! I am a *daughter of Abraham*," she said with a delightful chuckle. "And I think that may be where I get my wicked sense of humor."

I said, "I couldn't tell whether it was a comment on meats you didn't like or a comment on how much the two of us had eaten." I read her note out loud, "'Pigs get fat, hogs get slaughtered. Care to share some pastries, coffee, and good old USA laughter? Lou Abraham.'"

"Maybe it was both," she said with a smile as we joined her in laughter.

We sat for what must have been hours, three newfound friends lost together in time.

Lou had the most compelling combination of a brilliant mind, a quick wit, and an erudite demeanor. She was simply fun and fun loving, while oddly proper and prim.

As she and Doc discussed their mutual interest in physics, they began to act like long-lost friends—speaking the same language and discovering deeper levels of conversation, leaving me to sit and marvel at their intelligent dialogue.

As only a writer does, I took out my stub of a pencil along with my small notepad and began to record where their conversation was centered—much of which I did not grasp. I knew I could ask Doc later for clarity on all points not understood.

Doc and Lou had much in common. I was the safe third wheel that sat and observed a brilliant conversation unfold. She loved physics and was quite conversant in many fields about which I held only a cursory understanding but which Doc fully understood.

We learned that Lou Abraham's interest in German history and physics began initially as a personal interest in her uncle, Max Abraham. She'd met him when she was a young girl in 1909, and he left a lasting impression on her. He'd relocated from the University of Göttingen in Germany to the Urbana-Champaign area to teach at the University of Illinois. He quickly became disenchanted by the small-minded nature of Midwesterners as well as the even smaller size of the university. Having taught in Europe at a university that was founded in 1737 at the start of the Enlightenment, graduating among its illustrious alumni, Otto von Bismarck, he somehow thought this small, "unenlightened" university located not too far from the Great Lakes seemed just too small.

His American visit was cut short, as he opted instead to accept an invitation to move to Italy and teach at the University of Milan.

Lou's few months with this uncle left the little girl sure of a few things about him: he was very kind to her, and he was brilliant. Oh, there was a third thing: he deeply disliked a man named Einstein. As a little girl, she sat at her uncle's feet as he talked with adult family members who had previously emigrated from Germany.

He called her Lou and not her formal name. She liked that.

She listened to stories of the Germans and their kaiser, of science and light, of universities in Europe versus "little schools" (as he called them) in America. Lou heard her uncle Max speak of having been cheated by this man, Einstein, and somehow in her little girl mind, this cheater stole a *relative* ... or at least that's how it sounded to her.

Like a conquering hero, Max Abraham came, he saw, and he returned home to Europe. He wrote often to the little girl, having seen a sharp mind in her during his visit. His letters always began, "My little Lou."

Lou grew to maturity in Illinois, eventually attending and then graduating from *that little school*. She responded to her uncle's letters with questions of light and energy, of the physical world, and of space. Her course of education, so long ago introduced to her by that smart uncle, the internationally known physicist, Dr. Max Abraham, was only natural: physics.

For such a brief moment in time, his impact had light years of effect on her. Literally.

For postgraduate work, Lou studied abroad under Dr. Stefan Meyer at the University of Vienna for the academic year 1912–1913, working on various physics experiments while enjoying the lovely capital city of Austria. She enjoyed in particular her newfound taste for espresso coffee at a lovely café. Friends at the university told her that Café Central was a pleasant and warm place to meet friends indoors—especially during the extremely cold month of January.

Realizing that we had to send me on my way back to my Idaho townhouse via TC1, Doc and I excused ourselves by saying, "We have to go visit a place about a thing."

"Sounds intriguing and *very* American man-ish," she said, laughing. "Every time I hear my fellow countrymen describe that new sport in the USA—football—I hear them use equally obscure and vague language."

This time, I laughed. My wife had always complained that men speaking football lingo sounded much like cavemen. Apparently, there's something timeless to that.

We all agreed to meet again once I returned.

6

1913

"Where is it?" he asked as I suddenly reentered the library of 1913, after the trip to my townhouse in Idaho.

Shaking off the mind-numbing travel shock, I looked up and handed him my backpack of contraband I'd taken from the future.

I said, "I took a look at my security camera app before I left. I had a visitor when I was not there."

"You had a what?" Doc reacted in fear.

"Someone broke into my house, and my security camera caught him on video," I said nonchalantly, thinking that *I* should be more upset than my spacetime partner was. I added, "He was quite creepy to look at, but I checked, and he left my office unmolested."

I reached in my back pocket, unfolded the piece of paper with the picture of the thief on it, and moved to hand it to Doc. He grabbed it from me as he jumped up from his chair. He also grabbed the backpack and dumped it on the table, examining each book. His motions became quicker as he reviewed the books, looking back into the bag for something else. It apparently wasn't there.

"Really? Really?" repeated Doc. "Let's see how successful this thief really was," he said as he slapped the image on the table with one hand as he shifted the books around with his other hand.

"Doc? What's going on?" I reached over and retrieved the folded paper with the image.

"The signed copy of President Grant's book!" he shouted as he kept rummaging through the backpack. "It's not here." He sighed with disappointment. He stood up as if in a dream, looking at nothing in particular with glassy eyes.

I moved to the assortment of books now dumped out on the chair and picked up the copy of Grant's memoirs. "Here it is, Doc."

He looked at me and dismissed it with the wave of his hand. "That's volume 2, not volume 1." He paused, looked at me, and said in a monotone voice, "It's the unsigned copy. Only volume 1 has his autograph in it. You of all people know that."

I looked down at the book. He was right. I realized what I'd done. I had not stopped to think that only one book of the two-volume set was on my desk. I grabbed the single volume and put it in my backpack.

In doing so, I'd completely blown it.

"But," I said, "we have the other books, the other signatures, the other TCs."

"Yes, and my guess is that picture is of Lafayette Backus! *He* was your visitor. He now has the one book that counts: the volume that takes us—him—back to when his bother Orrin meets General Grant and opens the portal to where we wanted to meet and save General Sedgwick. He doesn't want that. He wants the Civil War to continue, and to do so, General Sedgwick must die. That changes everything," he said exhaustedly as he plopped down on the edge of his chair. "We won't be able to save his life and, through that, affect the sequence of events that will stop Hitler."

He continued, "Somehow in time and space, there is a chain of events that leads from Sedgwick's death to Hitler's rise. We're still searching them out, and we must change them! If we don't change them, Lafayette will keep history as is, stopping us from eliminating Hitler's power and his death grip on the world."

I sat down, not sure of the connection from John Sedgwick to Adolf Hitler, through this man with a difficult name, Ernst Hanfstaengl, as well as a goofy nickname: Putzi.

"Wait a minute." I turned toward him. "We have the signed copy of the book this guy Putzi wrote. We've already gone back to 1913. And if we can do that, we can *also* go forward in time to Putzi's life, meet him, find out about his namesake, and then return to 1864 using his book and the TC that runs through Berlin and save the general's life." I was becoming visibly excited at solving this.

He looked up at me, though not yet excited.

I continued, "Doc—you *really* don't mind me calling you Doc, do you?" He shook his head in an uncaring fashion, as though the situation had become hopeless in such a short period of time.

I continued, "I don't know how this whole dimensional travel thing works, but I have now experienced it twice, so I know that it does work. I'm ready to go with you on this next journey from 1913 to 1922, when Hitler was here in Vienna just about to meet Putzi. Since we understand that the travel process works, we *could* go that different direction."

I spoke slowly and carefully. "Can we do something before we go?"

Doc looked up at me. "Maybe. What do you have in mind?"

I amped up. "Can we just get positive? In order to do what needs to now be done, we've *got* to keep focused on what we *can* do, rather than what seems impossible at the moment." My mind was racing, as was my heart.

I wanted him to understand this other option from someone's perspective who had lost something deeply through death and yet stayed positive and responsive rather than reactive and fearful. "Look, if there's breath, there's hope," I said as I ended my brief tirade.

Doc rose to his feet and, turning to me, said, "You're correct. We must now go in a different direction. The key to our travel is to define what our goals are so that plan B meets every aspect of what will accomplish what I wanted in plan A."

He picked up the book by Putzi. "Let's see. *Hitler: The Missing Years.*" He turned to the signature located in the front of the book and studied it.

"Author, allow me to go deeper with you on my research and what it is that ultimately we must do, so that we'll both be on the same page for the plan."

He seemed completely back with me now, even slightly smiling as he turned toward me.

I smiled back at him.

He moved his hands as a conductor would. "Lafayette Backus supposedly died on November 14, 1914. A headstone in Columbus, Ohio, notes the date. However, after Orrin moved from Ohio to California, his brother continued on with their family business for only a very short time until he too moved to join his brother in Southern California. I was able to find out, going through his family's papers, that both brothers made a tremendous amount of money in the years after the Civil War, clear up to the turn of the century. They started banks, their businesses grew, and strangely enough, both men became self-taught agronomists—scientists trying to devise methods to increase crop yield—specifically focusing on orange trees and vineyards for raisins. Because of them, the orange and citrus industries still exist in Southern California."

"They both must have become so wealthy," I remarked and nodded at him to continue. He motioned for me to take my seat, as though a lecture was to begin.

He continued, "Indeed they did. At some point during the first decade of the new century, Lafayette's interest in science turned away from Orrin's and toward the greater works of scientific inquiry. In 1909, he met German scientist Max Abraham, the uncle of our new female friend from Café Central, during an agricultural visit to the University of Illinois, where, as Lou explained, Abraham was a visiting professor, and was captivated by Abraham's intellect as he sat in on a lecture on the combined elements of velocity and particle matter.

"Abraham, a disciple of Max Planck, was only at the university a matter of months and decided to return to Germany. Backus saw this as a fortunate meeting and soon caught up with him in Europe."

My head became cloudy with so many facts. "Where are you going with this?" I asked.

"My dear Author." He smiled. "It's called background."

He continued, "In December 1911, Abraham published a significant paper with the financial support of Lafayette Backus. It seems that Abraham and Albert Einstein had become involved in a rather public debate on an integral issue of the relationship between the velocity of light and gravitational potential. Abraham accused Einstein of 'borrowing' his equations without approval. I suppose that's a scientist's way of yelling 'thief.'"

I nodded, beginning to put the pieces together. "And turning a little girl named Lou into one of the few Einstein haters of all time. This sounds pretty intense."

"It is. Although the issue of their debate itself in 1911 and 1912 doesn't matter to us right now, what matters is that Backus took the side of Max Abraham and invested in his work and stood against Albert Einstein."

"Doc, you didn't say any of this to Lou when we were together at Café Central."

"I know."

"But why not?"

Dr. Gersema looked past me and was quiet for just a few seconds. Then he stated, "Once Lou mentioned her uncle's name, I had to arrest my enthusiasm and be cautious. Although she's a brilliant and young postgraduate student, I needed to know if she was in any way involved with Lafayette Backus's still-unfolding plan."

"Is she?" I asked.

He shook his head side to side. "My guess is that it's purely coincidental that we met at the café." He paused once again, and then, as if regaining his enthusiasm, he said, "But we can certainly make it strategically important for us to continue meeting young Miss Abraham." He seemed to have other thoughts occurring as he spoke.

Dr. Gersema continued telling me about Dr. Abraham and his relationship with Dr. Einstein. "Lafayette Backus's close relationship with Abraham allowed him access to the studies, the books, and the personal tutoring that Planck had made available in the early years. In time, Max Abraham developed the initial signs of a brain tumor, so Backus took over more and more of the theoretical studies on dimensional travel and light, while having the finances to support the work alongside others. Abraham passed away due to the tumor, and Backus continued the experiments. Few knew of his work. I only found out due to the odd factoid that his name came up in historical documents two years after Lafayette Backus supposedly died."

"You mean he did not die?" I questioned.

Doc just raised his eyebrows, nodded, and said, "Author, this man is an evil fellow. Think of it, to have the capacity to go back through the ages and stop Adolf Hitler—and refusing to do so. Because of that, he may be even more vile than Hitler."

He looked down at the floor and uttered, "Yeah, about Hitler ..."

"What?" I responded.

"I think we should do something before we head forward to 1922 when Putzi meets Hitler."

"Okay. What?"

He looked up and said, "I want us to try something before we expend the energy of heading to 1922. I want us both to process the most obvious thing that needs to be done in our current situation, since Lafayette Backus has the signed Grant volume."

I nodded. "Okay. What are you thinking?"

"I want *us* to meet Adolf Hitler."

"What?"

A long pause enveloped the two of us.

"I want to try a scientific inquiry—a method of sorts—to see what will happen," he stated matter-of-factly.

We simply looked at each other. I wasn't at all sure what he was talking about, and that was par for the course, I had come to understand, so I shrugged and just said, "Okay. When we return, can we send a card over to where Lou is staying to set up a next time for the three of us to grab a meal and talk?"

He said, "Yes, but first, let's go meet Der Führer."

As was my new 1913 domestic custom, I grabbed his coat and mine, handing Doc's to him.

It seemed heavier than before.

Young Adolf Hitler's residence was located at Meldemannstrasse 27 in Vienna's twentieth district, just a little over a mile away from Café Central. It was the kind of group home that self-styled bohemians exist in while trying to pretend they're successful to potential clients.

Hitler's childhood is the goldmine about which future Freudians will, after his death, collectively spend millions of hours researching, then publish an untold amount of titles and tomes. They'll repeatedly ask similar versions of the same question: how did he become a monster?

But those days are many decades in front of him.

In 1913, he was merely a painter hoping to become an art student, living in Vienna, oddly enough just walking distance from Dr. Sigmund Freud's own fledgling practice.

Adolf saw himself as an architectural artist, making a living painting postcards and selling them to locals and tourists. On this day in January 1913, he was alone and lonely—in search of an identity, in search of friends.

Our knock on his door was met with silence.

Then, slowly, the door opened, and standing before us was the young man himself: Adolf Hitler.

"Guten Tag. What may I do for you?" he said.

The sudden and pungent smell of blood and gunpowder stunned me.

I can barely describe the emotions that coursed through my mind.

Fear took immediate root, spreading like an emotional uncorking of shock, dread, and self-defense—all at once, all together. Another human being killed right before my eyes, his brains blown against the white clapboard wall. Eight rounds? Six rounds? One round was all it took, but the need to ensure the complete, sudden, yet unexpected destruction of a monster in training seemed to demand an empty magazine by the killer.

The body of Adolf Hitler lay before me, lifeless and futureless.

Russ Gersema slowly and methodically picked up the spent shell casings, placing each in his left coat pocket as he held the pistol in his right. I slumped against the doorway as though my legs were about to give out on me.

He turned to me and simply said, "We have seven minutes to return to my flat before the police arrive." Reaching over to steady me, he led me into the dank, empty hallway to begin our retreat. I looked around, worried that someone would open a door, peer through, and take note of our faces.

"No one is here," the killer stated matter-of-factly. "I knew he'd be alone."

Somehow, the simple words of *alone* and *he* and *no one* all combined with those pungent odors to create an immediate world where normal things described the cruelest of all abnormal things: the death of a human being.

He steadied me by my left elbow and ushered us both down the small stairs and out a side exit onto a street bustling with Austrians out in the cold winter morning, living, walking, and being. I momentarily glanced back at the window of the room of the nonbeing, where I thought we had just been. We walked on.

The theory that spacetime is relative showed itself to me as footfalls sounded and turned corners were met and conquered at moderate speeds by a man guiding me. Time sped by as it stood still. The white flat with its blue-stained stairs quickly met us, reminding me of the white and red wall we'd just left.

My killer-helper unlocked the door and guided me into the hallway and onto the swooning couch. I slumped down on it, fully clothed, lying in my heavy wool coat, gloves, and utter shock.

He soon knelt down and handed me a pill in one hand and a glass of water in the other. "Take this; you've been through a lot." I obeyed.

My eyelids grew heavy. I could hear in the distant background a police siren, but my senses slowly ceased altogether.

My unprescribed sleep treatment eventually ended, and I stirred myself, sans wool fabrics and wooly memory. I had no idea how many hours I had slept.

I walked into the library and made my way to the plush sofa chair, quietly placing myself directly in the line of sight of Dr. Russell Gersema, the assassin of Adolf Hitler. He was reading a book.

Looking up, he smiled.

"Well, we had to get that off the table right away, didn't we?"

I recoiled and found my voice, which grew louder.

"You never told me that we were headed to his house to blow off his head!"

"Author, Author, please allow me to explain."

I wouldn't allow him to say anything.

"I know he was Hitler, but he had done nothing … yet."

Gersema the assassin held up his right hand, like a traffic cop in any city at any crosswalk. In it was his weapon.

I stopped any further rant.

He saw my look.

"It's still empty," he said, slowly bringing it to the table next to him. "Now that I have your attention, I will explain what we did today."

"What *you* did today," I said.

He smiled the smile of an almost-kind man. I shuddered.

"Author, I want you to willingly suspend your disbelief about what *I* did—what you saw me do. I also apologize for not telling you beforehand."

I stared at him as he continued.

"You and I could have debated at length which direction to take as we reviewed the options for history, right?"

I nodded, listening.

"And the one option almost every single person in the twentieth and twenty-first centuries would have chosen was to do what I did—whether Hitler was at the top of his power during World War II or if it was years before his ascending the power pyramid of the National Socialist Party."

I interrupted. "Yeah, both were *after* he had begun killing ..."

Gersema held up his hand, this time without the Steyr-Mannlicher in it.

"Please." He nodded, his line of sight under his arched brows directly focused at me. "Please don't interrupt."

I acknowledged his civil request. He was, after all, a *civil* assassin, I thought.

He seemed to sense my internal debate. "It's okay to feel the way you feel right now. It's a confused feeling, but please hang on, and we'll get past this. I'd like to put this into perspective."

He paused, took a long sip from that crystal tumbler of his, ice clinking and the golden hue of liquor swirling down the side of the glass and past his large moustache.

"Ahh, here goes," he began, placing the tumbler on the top of the half bookcase.

"Killing Hitler stopped World War II, correct?"

I was put off by his justified question, yet it made sense to ask it.

He continued, "That's what you and I, as well as many others, would naturally think. History's view of Hitler is horribly accurate because he was a terrible monster, his worldview even more monstrous than he. Ending his life would most assuredly end what he did to the six million Jews and over thirty-four million others who died as military and civilian victims."

Doc paused. "And yet ..." He looked out the window at the January cold of Vienna. "There remain a cabal of others who actually killed more than the Austrian painter killed. All of them remain alive."

I thought of Café Central.

"History's Lenin, Trotsky, Tito, and Stalin together saw more than twenty-six million of their fellow citizens die as a result of their war policies—among those, 8.7 million soldiers. Some Russian historians count ancillary deaths, bringing the overall total dead to forty million men, women, and children. That's roughly 15 percent of the USSR's population. And none of those figures take into account the *enemies* they killed. All because of the men who this month sit together at a café in our city, not having yet been introduced to one another."

I sat, measuring the words he used and the words he didn't use.

"Author, today I ended the life of one man and saved the lives of six million. What would it be like if someone ended the lives of all of those men and saved forty million others while doing so?"

He seemed almost too energized, too intense, but at the same time too embarrassed. There was something hidden in his comments, something I couldn't quite grasp.

I decided to enter into that fog and into his embarrassment.

"What about the value of one person's life, Doc? What about the value of *each* man's life inside Café Central?" My questions seemed more like simple, factual statements than they were attempts at questioning the human value of killing Hitler.

His reaction caught me by surprise.

He smiled and said, "That's another reason why I brought you into this situation, Author. I need to hear *and see* the larger ethical arguments you present, because—more than you are aware of as we sit here today—there is an unethical player in this drama, and I could easily see that perspective regarding the destruction *or* protection of these men."

I winced, trying to understand who this other player was.

He kept on as if to no one. "It was so very easy for me to squeeze off the rounds back in that room, so very easy. As a Jew, I had to."

7

1913 Becomes
the Present

I sat stunned.

Realizing that he had never referred to his nationality before, Doc looked up at me and continued almost in a stream of consciousness, "My family is Jewish, none practicing or connected to our grandfather's faith he had when he died in Dachau. We're just Jews—like so many who *were to be* murdered by that man whose life I ended. They will now live because he died."

He paused once more and then breathed a deep sigh. "It is vital we return to the present to see just how successful the world is now and ... to meet my family. To see Israel."

He looked at the frayed edges of the throw rug beneath our feet and cupped his chin in his right hand as his elbow rested on his knee.

Then, as if slowly awakening, he asked, "May I see your book, Author?"

I handed him my copy of *A Change of Time*. He opened it to the signature page and stared at me, motioning for me to join him in standing up. Together, we walked to the portion of the library from which I had not so recently transferred through spacetime to something then called the present.

Neither of us said a word. He opened the flyleaf page, where we placed our hands on my signature and stepped together onto what we came to call TC1—the telluric current that hurled us forward to the lives we both had, to a future we'd never had. We closed our eyes.

The whoosh of spacetime is indescribable. It's not like *anything* in our experiential world—not like a rushing wind, or the sound near an opening to a tunnel. It simply is a moment of time that *is*. It is how the prophet Moses described the name of his God—I Am. One moment, we were. The next moment, we are.

There can be a sort of fuzziness attached to the travel, but even that word is inconsequential to describe the effect and aftereffect of travel through spacetime via telluric current.

We opened our eyes to a world the way we both wanted it to be, even if, for me, it had cost the ghastly face-to-face murder of one man over a century (or a quarter hour) ago.

The first thing I noticed was that everything was normal. My companion in spacetime travel and I were standing in the front area of my Idaho townhouse, the Boise River rolling gently behind us. We stepped out of the TC pathway and over to my garage door. I keyed in my code, and the large door obediently opened. We moved past my Saturn Sky roadster and the empty slot where my wife's car use to be parked, in through the house doorway. As we walked in, nothing of notice had changed.

Doc broke the silence. "Kinda refreshing that it's all so normal."

I smiled as we both walked upstairs to my office.

He nodded, then added with a smile, "I hope we never get used to spacetime traveling."

"Spacetime traveling? Is that what we're calling this? Ha, that's a mouthful, but I suppose I like it."

I glanced over at the desk with all my normal items of life and then froze.

Doc noticed. "What is it?"

I pointed wide-eyed at the picture from my past of my wife with her fifth-grade students, propped up on my desk. It was the typical elementary school photo of a teacher and her students saluting the flag.

Only in this version, all the students and their teacher, smiling, had their arms stretched out in the "Heil, Hitler" salute.

My whole body began to shake. *My wife. This salute? What the …*

"Well, that's interesting," Doc casually commented as he placed his hand on my shaking forearm to settle me down. "Let's go out and discover more."

We exited through my front door and headed on foot down the greenbelt—a stretch of land deeded to the local municipality by homeowners on the edge of the Boise River that allows others to freely walk down the side of this lovely river, enjoying the beauty and natural wildness that is Idaho. It runs adjacent to my townhouse.

Just a little less than a half mile away sits a coffee shop that I use for writing or meeting people. I suppose we both needed time to process that photograph and for Doc to give me further thoughts on what we might find.

"Now, Author, don't get too confused about your wife's class photo."

"Oh, you mean the photo where all the junior Nazis are saluting the American flag along with their Nazi teacher, my dead wife? That photo?" I asked.

He looked at me with a side glance and then kept talking as we walked. "My best guess is that *that* was not what it appeared to be. Remember the Bellamy salute? You know, the pre-World War II flag salute used by Americans that looked remarkably like the Hitler salute?"

I nodded.

"Look, in this dimension, there is no Adolf Hitler, never was. Well, at least to anyone other than his family. He died a long time ago. Der Führer's salute never was used in Germany because there was never a Führer and never a top psychopath to demand such a display of allegiance. Instead, it continued to be used for decades in America—ever since the late 1800s. The photo just proves Hitler's lack of impact."

I thought, *It still looks hideous.*

"Did you grab your iPhone at your house, as I earlier requested?" he asked, breaking my train of thought.

"I did. It was on my desk near the photo."

"Google 'Nazi' for me."

The familiar iPhone, so much a part of my life in the past, felt odd in my hand in the present. It was less of a chic, trim style and more of a flat, military grade, smaller version of the phone. I touched the screen to go online, as per Doc's request.

There was no "online."

"Doc, this is just a cell phone—certainly not the iPhone I had before."

"Hmm," is all he said, furrowing his brow and picking up the pace as we made it closer to the Bistro, my neighborhood coffee shop.

Deep in thought, we both moved as a small unit, saying nothing for a few minutes, when Dr. Russell Gersema—noted physicist and spacetime traveler—stopped cold, turned to me, and said, "There could be another reason for the phone."

I looked on, expecting him to continue.

He didn't.

Something had caught his eye up ahead.

The last stretch of the walk to the Bistro was quickly accomplished, although I noticed that as we approached it, the name had been changed.

The sign was in a Deutsche Schrift font with English spelling.

As we entered, the young female barista smiled and greeted us. "Welcome to the Burgerbrau Cellar. May I help you?"

We walked to the counter and ordered an espresso and a hot chocolate.

Then I asked, "Why did you change the business name?"

She flickered her eyes in a questioning way, paused, and then responded, "I've worked here since it was built. It's always been the Burgerbrau Cellar."

"You sell burgers with your coffee now?" I paused, then quickly added, "And why 'cellar'? This place is a one-story structure. There's no basement."

Her professionally welcoming demeanor was changing, and she seemed to think this might be a joke. "Silly, *Herr*, you know that all the coffeehouses in the country carry this name. We originated in Seattle, and we're everywhere. And no, we don't sell hamburgers, but we sell beer—nice Bavarian beer."

Doc and I looked at each other.

I continued, "And *cellar*?"

She tossed down her white drying towel and leaned over the backside of the coffee bar toward me, "Failed gymnasium history, did you?"

Doc interrupted. "Author, grab up a couple of newspapers over there." He was pointing at the usual pile of read-and-discarded papers off to the side. Out of earshot of the barista, he said, "We need to see what this new world is about."

He found an empty table.

The hot beverages arrived, and I gathered the newspapers together—odds and ends from many different publishers. They were strange newspaper names that I had never before seen.

Doc read through the front page of one called the *Mirror*. "Nothing is familiar," he said, almost to himself.

I turned the pages of another newspaper, the *Image*, and read an editorial about an upcoming celebration, on November 28, called Founders Day. In part it read:

We're all very grateful for the incredible
work that The Founder did for us. Ernst
Röhm's contributions years ago to the work of
combining the nationalists and the socialists
in America will always be celebrated from
the Blue Mountains of West Vahala over the
Rockies to the shores of San Thulecisco. May
his name remain honored.

I sipped my hot chocolate, which was as wonderful as what
I had enjoyed in Vienna at Café Central. I turned to Doc and
handed him his espresso and my editorial. He received both yet
was immersed in his own article. He folded the newspaper he was
reading, then read mine while taking short sips of coffee. When
finished, Russ Gersema seemed to have a gleam in his eye as he
straightened up and walked over to the barista.

"Hi there, may I ask you a question or two ... Vanessa?" he
said, reading the name tag of the conservatively dressed, young
blonde woman behind the counter.

She looked back at him very seriously. "Yes, certainly."

"What day is November 28 in American history?"

She paused and took inventory of my friend. "What? C'mon,
I thought you were serious."

She finished wiping dry a glass coffee mug and placed it on
the counter. "Everyone knows what day that is!" she said with a
disparaging throwaway glance toward him.

"Please forgive me; I'm not from around here."

"Oh, from Canada, *eh*?" She chuckled at her failed attempt
of an accent.

Doc gave her a courtesy smile. "Canada ..."

She continued, "Don't give me that. You know there is no
Canada. There's only the northernmost states of the American
Reich."

Doc and I looked at each other again then back to her.

I barely squeaked out, "And why is that date celebrated?"

She really looked bothered, this time at me.

"It's the celebration of the birth of the Founder!"

I looked blank, as did Doc.

The silence was a new guest to our conversation.

She continued, "Ernst Röhm … you know, *the Founder!*" As she exclaimed this, she pointed to the sepia-toned photograph on the wall of a man from the 1920s. Large and brutish, he sat for the portrait in a type of storm trooper's uniform. Under his portrait was a large leather-bound book—laid out as a religious person might display a Bible.

"Every kid in America knows Ernst Röhm," she volunteered, making the long *o* sound even longer.

Then she nonchalantly said as though it was no big deal, "He completely got rid of the damn Jews in America." She smiled and asked us if we wanted refills. Then she added, "Only those small bands of terrorists in the nation of Palestine still exist. But they'll soon be gone too …" Her voice trailed off as she picked up another glass to dry.

"May I take a look at the bound book under the portrait?" Doc asked, hiding his utter shock.

"Certainly," she answered. "Maybe it'll help you with your American history!"

The book was titled *My Conquest*. He opened the book; it was in English. I looked over his shoulder.

The inscription read, "Ernst Röhm, the Founder of the National Socialist movement, the hero of the Great Peace, the champion of the Small War, and modern day's George Washington for the New Reich."

Together we digested the book from start to finish—hours later handing it back to Vanessa, having emptied all of her many liquid refills.

I stopped at one point to visit the restroom. "Vanessa, where is the men's room?"

She looked back at me rather oddly.

"The what?"

"The men's room? The toilet?" I responded in a needful state of urgency.

"Oh, the water closet! It's down the hall to the right."

Then, as if to attempt her hand at humor again, she added, "Women and others can use it too."

The entire afternoon was surreal. Real but not real. There but not there. This America was not the country into which I had been born.

As we ended the afternoon there, we stood to exit—not quite knowing exactly to where we'd be exiting.

"Hope it helped!" she exclaimed as we opened the front door and left. We nodded.

"Doc, how did that happen? We, er, you killed Hitler!"

Keeping his calm as we walked back toward the greenbelt, Gersema recounted the facts. "I killed Hitler; you are correct. I didn't kill Nazism. Ernst Röhm took credit for cofounding the Nazi Party in 1919 with a man named Herr Buche Backhaus, just before Hitler became a member of it. Röhm was a street thug and a very violent man, having learned his craft in World War I. He also founded the Brown Shirts—Hitler's goon squad that bullied, terrorized, and then murdered many of those who publicly opposed Hitler. In fact, Röhm was the only one of the top Nazis who did not use the title Der Führer when he addressed him; he simply called him Adolf.

"In our previous dimension, Hitler had Röhm arrested on or about July 1, 1934, for treason and then had him murdered in his cell just after the Night of the Long Knives in Munich. But in this dimension, Hitler died early and Röhm lived long."

He stopped as if to take in the irony.

Then he continued, "And he became the Founder of the Nazi political movement, living until 1987, when he died in

Palm Springs, California, where he passed away in his sleep on November 28, his hundredth birthday."

"Did you see what that book said he accomplished in those one hundred years?" I asked.

"Indeed, I did."

I looked at the notes I'd jotted down in the coffee shop and continued speaking as we walked. "In 1908, at twenty-one years old, Röhm was commissioned as an officer in the Royal Bavarian Tenth Infantry Regiment and by 1913 was fully skilled at the art of soldiering and killing. He was prepared for war yet brokered with monarchies what they referred to as the Great Peace. He played the peacemaker yet murdered those who would not agree with him. Through deceit, bribery, and an accurate hunting style, he succeeded in finding what he called 'hives of communists' and killing them, almost for pleasure."

Doc said, "Almost?"

"Okay, for pleasure. Did you read what it was he blew up in Vienna in late January 1913 just prior to a war starting? He destroyed Café Central, *our* Café Central. The news articles called it the Red Morning." I looked at my notes once again. "It was the day he and that man named Herr Buche Backhaus murdered local communists as well as rescued royalty at the café. Pure personal advancement. Pure luck. Pure murder."

I looked at him as I said it. He didn't look back at me.

I continued, "Since he blew up Café Central, it would have been historically convenient for him and his friend to have killed Lenin, Stalin, and Trotsky all at one time. The victims were nobodies to the press, just communists. The newspapers showed how the two heroes rescued both Emperor Franz Josef and Archduke Franz Ferdinand, who were also at the café and barely injured. That would explain how quickly he rose in the Austro-Hungarian Army. In his heroic acts, he also ensured the czar's continuance on the Russian throne. He could have killed the men who would later kill the czar and his family."

I felt pretty full of myself, pretty confident.

"Röhm and his friend *did* kill Stalin, Lenin, Tito, and Trotsky," Doc said flatly as we walked.

"We don't know that for sure; none of the names mentioned were familiar, let alone pronounceable," I mockingly admonished.

He unfolded his note paper and read: "'The bodies of thirty-four-year-old Stavros Papadopoulos, forty-three-year-old Vladimir Ilyich Ulyanov, twenty-one-year old Josip Broz, and thirty-five-year-old Lev Davidovich Bronstein were found in the charred debris of Café Central in Vienna yesterday, January 18, 1913.'" Then he paused. "Stalin, Lenin, Tito, and Trotsky."

I shut up.

I'm always amazed at Dr. Gersema. He finds gems where few see them—okay, where I fail to see them.

Doc added, "Röhm apparently cofounded the Nazi Party six years earlier—in 1913—than he did in our spacetime dimension. As a Nazi, *the* very founder of the Nazi Party, through these acts of murder, he was able to stop World War I and create a false peace, until, how did that book say it?"

I answered, "They called it the Great Peace, and I saw a section that read, 'Until the Western powers dishonored the pure monarchies of continental Europe,' I think is how the book phrased it. Think of it: one half of the National Socialist Party was made up of a party of monarchy nationals who combined with the other lesser party, the socialists, to give a majority of 51 percent to their combined government in the Reichstag. Hitler never did that; he only accomplished a plurality of 43.9 percent, and it took him fourteen additional years to take over. Röhm built it in a day."

I was hoping to make Doc smile with my self-appraised clever twist of the obvious phrase.

He smirked, which was good enough for both of us at this point.

My smirk turned to sadness as I continued. "And the way he and this coconspirator, Herr Backhaus, developed a group of commando terrorists that attacked America, France, and England, using mustard gas to annihilate so many in each nation's capital, is terrible yet remarkable: three combined simultaneous strikes, three weak governments unable to match his combined Central European armies, two dead prime ministers, and one dead US president. After that, he broke the will of each nation and built several death camps throughout the defeated countries."

Doc added, "Röhm took over by advancing peace in Europe, then finding common enemies—the Western powers, England, France, and America—blaming them for a series of events and attacking them. A classic Nazi move. It was deceit, brute force, and subjugation. This Herr Backhaus became Röhm's deputy commander and began the systematic killing of Americans, state by state. His level of evil was greater than even what Hitler's deputies did in the original Third Reich's reign of terror—and he did it to Americans in small towns and large cities—against people of faith. People of all faiths, certainly Jews but also Christians and Muslims, Mormons, Jehovah Witnesses, and many Eastern faiths. His goal was total elimination of believers in every religious faith. By all accounts from what we've just read, he succeeded."

We walked on, silently.

"Our killing of Hitler only killed one man—not the idea. Röhm used this philosophy to kill millions and create a Reich that spanned the oceans rather than a thousand years," I said.

As we walked past the municipal police station, we noticed that the flagpole held an unfurled red, white, and blue flag, but no stars and stripes were evident on it. In their place was a series of red, white, and blue swastikas—by my guess, fifty-plus.

"Think of it, Author. We couldn't Google any of this, because the two founders of Google never lived. Larry Page's mother was Jewish, and both of Sergey Brin's parents were Russian Jews. The parents must have been killed, so their sons were never born."

I added, "And no nation of Israel or an Albert Einstein, no Max and no Lou Abraham, no Simon Wiesenthal, no Louis

Mayer or Steven Spielberg, no Arthur Miller and no Jerry Siegel and Joe Shuster."

Doc seemed particularly reactive when I said, "No Lou Abraham," though he recovered quickly, almost embarrassed.

Doc kept wincing, failing to understand the final two names. "No Sigel and Shuster ... um, who are they?"

"Well, if we had Google, you'd know in a moment, but ..." I toyed with him.

I pointed up into the air with a mock sense of urgency. "Look up in the sky. It's a bird, it's a plane, it's ..."

Doc smiled.

I concluded, "No Superman, no Google, no special or general theory of relativity, no Israel."

Doc added, "What a dull, stupid gray world this is, spellbound under the global dominance of two diplomatically clever mass murderers."

"This isn't Hitler; it's doubly worse than what Hitler delivered," I said as we came around the greenbelt's corner near my townhouse.

Then he froze.

He turned to me and asked me to once again say the name of Röhm's coconspirator.

I replied, "Buche Backhaus."

Mining the depths of his German and French vocabularies, Doc looked off to the horizon, crunching nouns, crunching thoughts.

I stood waiting.

Then he announced quite simply, "Buche in English means beech—as in the beech tree forests of Germany. In French, beech tree forests originated from the words *la faieta*. And from that came the name *lafayette*."

He continued, "Backhaus in German becomes Backus in English."

"Lafayette Backus!" I exclaimed.

Turning to me, with fear in his voice, Doc said, "We've got to leave right now."

I pulled out my copy of *A Change of Time*, and we stood in place to do just that.

8

1913

In writing, successfully great people are taught to avoid their comfort zones.

In dimensional spacetime travel, I've learned the opposite—that successfully embracing comfort zones can have great merit.

Vienna in 1913 was—for the most part—comfortable.

Arriving back in Vienna in early January, Dr. Russell Gersema and I found ourselves once more in the frigid temperatures of a harsh European winter—in which still lived Adolf Hitler.

And, *strangely*, we were comfortable.

There was no Founder; nor was there yet a Führer. Ernst Röhm was alive, as was Hitler, though they had yet to meet for several more years. Nazism was six years away from existing.

There *still* was Lafayette Backus though—out there, preparing his own plans, almost outside of spacetime, able to enter in as he pleased.

Odd as it was, Doc and I had *still* just met earlier that day, though I was completely conscious and aware of all the days, months, and years through which we had now traveled together.

"I see what you earlier meant when you talked about reading my books, yet we'd met only minutes before," I said, trying to break the ice surrounding our return.

We both plopped down in our chairs in the library.

He responded, "Yes, it's hard to believe we've been where we've been together and seen what we've seen."

"So, how does it really work?" I asked.

"What do you mean?"

I clarified my fuzzy question. "How are we transported through spacetime over great distances?"

I paused and looked directly at him. "I mean, putting my hand on my signature and standing on a tin foil hat ley line just seems, I don't know, *foolish*. What a strange way to move through dimensions and time."

"It's a telluric current," he said, distancing his work *again* from all the people who pretend to ignore the science in science-fiction. "Not a ley line."

He returned a steady line of sight to me. "And I can assure you, Author, that there's solid science behind our experiences, if you have an interest in entering once more into those subjects in your college years you seemed reticent to study."

"You mean like calculus?" I responded.

"And physics," he said.

"Okay, let's engage in this discussion—if you have the energy, I mean."

Doc smiled that broad smile of his and said, "First, let me do something I should have done a while ago."

He raised himself from the large chair and walked over to the bottle of liquor on the shelf. Cradling it in his right arm, he carried it to the nineteenth-century version of a wet bar sink. To my surprise, after dislodging the cork, he poured it down the drain.

"We'll need all of our wits to move forward, and this would have hindered me," he said, placing the now-empty bottle and its cap into the trash basket.

"So, who discovered calculus, dear Author?"

"Charles Manson?" I said with obvious relish and a slight hint of my known prejudice against the subject.

Doc did not react but continued.

"Isaac Newton. He was in a difficult time of life, working on a particularly grueling theory, and had to find a way of presenting a way in which he could implement a method to solve his overall problem. So he invented calculus."

Even hearing the word sent memory shivers down my backbone.

He continued, "Newton was brilliant. His contemporaries saw him as such; those who succeeded him in research and experiments felt they only accomplished what they did in their lifetimes because of this single man."

"That's quite a statement."

"Yes, it is. And it was expressed often by many other brilliant scientists and researchers in subsequent centuries." He crossed his legs, placing his hands together in an almost reverential, prayerlike way. "Isaac Newton was praised by no less a luminary than Albert Einstein."

"Really?"

"Oh yes. There are two known remarkable documents still in existence that Einstein penned in his lifetime involving Isaac Newton," Dr. Gersema said. "May I read one to you?"

"By all means," I said.

"It's a long one," he said, almost apologetically.

"Doc, no pun intended, but *we've got time.*"

He reached across the half bookshelf next to his chair to the assortment of important books and papers, part of his 1913 life. I noticed the books I'd brought back from my first visit to my home office were all nicely aligned, side by side.

He pulled out some loose linen sheets of paper that had typing on them.

"Okay, here goes," he said as if strapping the two of us into some type of rocket ship. "Credit goes to the Royal Society of Great Britain for making this available to the general public."

I chuckled to myself and thought, *What a brilliant man, about to read a series of thoughts written by another brilliant man about* the most *brilliant man who ever lived in modern history.*

Doc continued, "Einstein wrote this in 1927 as a eulogy to Newton on the bicentennial of Newton's death."

He began: "'He was not only an inventor of genius in respect of particular guiding methods; he also showed a unique mastery of the empirical material known in his time, and he was marvelously inventive in special mathematical and physical demonstrations. Causality—'"

I interrupted. "What does he mean?"

Doc looked over the top of the papers as a professor would approvingly look toward a lower-standing student who had just asked a wise question. He smiled.

"The relationship between cause and effect. It's the principle that everything has a cause."

"Thank you. Please continue."

He found his place in the document.

"'Newton's aim was to find an answer to the question: Does there exist a simple rule by which the motion of the heavenly bodies of our planetary system can be completely calculated, if the state of motion of all these bodies at a single moment is known?'"

I couldn't take it, even in so short a period of time. "I'm getting lost *already*. What is Einstein saying about Newton?"

Doc looked at me, picked up a pencil from next to him, and gently tossed it into the air, following it with his eyes as it fell to the floor.

"Gravity, Author! Gravity. Listen to Einstein: 'It was, no doubt, especially impressive to learn that the cause of the movements of the heavenly bodies is identical with the force of gravity so familiar to us from everyday experience.

"'The differential law is the form, which alone entirely satisfies the modern physicist's requirement of causality. The clear conception of the differential law is one of the greatest of Newton's intellectual achievements. What was needed was not only the idea but a formal mathematical method that was, indeed, extant in rudiment but had still to gain a systemic shape.

"'This also Newton found in the differential and integral ... calculus.'"

Doc stopped, looked over his glasses at me, and smiled the smile of a medical doctor finding a pain point, then continued. I caught his point and cringed.

"Doc, you're killing me."

"You mean that Einstein is killing you?"

"Okay, Einstein, Newton, and all your other buddies are killing *and* losing me," I stated with no emotion yet with a desire to follow the thought patterns.

"I'll unpack this at the end." He paused, lifting up his eyebrows. Suddenly finding something painfully funny to toss in my direction, he said, "There will be a test on this when I'm done."

My moans followed him as he laughed and continued. His reading of this eulogy dissertation continued for almost fifteen minutes. I caught some key points, and others simply alluded me. I knew though that we were nearing the end, and that meant a summary was due.

The doctor would soon be unpacking his patient's bandages from the calculus wound.

He read on. "'But owing to the barrenness, or at least the unfruitfulness, of these efforts there gradually occurred, after the end of the 19th century, a revulsion in fundamental conceptions; theoretical physics outgrew Newton's framework, which had for nearly two centuries provided fixity and intellectual guidance for science.'"

I interrupted again. "So Newton's work was not accurate?"

The good doctor corrected me. "Newton's work was not *complete*. Einstein almost completed the direction of Newton regarding gravity, heavenly bodies, and the spacetime nature of energy, equaling mass times the speed of light squared."

"$E = MC^2$? That's how Einstein improved on Newton's scientific observations?"

"Yes, energy equals mass times the speed of light, squared. This is anchored to his theories of general relativity and special relativity. Listen to how Einstein summarizes his differences with Newton."

Choosing excerpts near the end of the eulogy, Doc finished by reading in an excited voice, "'The last step in the development of the program of the field theory was the general theory of relativity. Space and time were so divested, not of their reality, but of their causal absoluteness, which Newton was compelled to attribute to them in order to be able to give expression to the laws then known.

"'From this short characterization it is clear how the elements of Newton's theory passed over into the general theory of relativity. The whole development of our ideas concerning natural phenomena may be conceived as an organic development of Newton's thought.'"

He folded the thick manuscript in half and placed it on his side table.

"Well. Author, Newton had an absolute scientific worldview, upon which Einstein built his relative worldview. And still those two worldviews were not complete. Remember Brian Green's work, *The Elegant Universe*?"

I nodded as if to say, "Of course I do." The 1999 book was resting on his 1913 table, along with my other books.

"It's because of Dr. Greene's book detailing both of these worldviews that I was able to build on Newton and Einstein's work—even going beyond what these three brilliant men could ever have conceived of."

"You mean spacetime travel—the very thing of here and now," I said in a hushed yet intense tone.

"Yes." He continued, "I've not only stood on the shoulders of Newton, Einstein, and Greene to peer into the future, but *we've* been jettisoned at light speeds high into the air far above them to see the past."

I added, "You may still need the help of Max Abraham and, more importantly, Lou Abraham to accomplish what we want."

He looked at me and slowly nodded his head in agreement.

We both solemnly paused, taking in this critical moment of understanding; it was something that no two people in the history of the human race had ever understood from science.

I looked up. One additional question forced its way from my lips. Almost embarrassed at breaking the solemnity of the moment, I said, "I understand the acceleration of speed, mass, and energy; what I don't understand is the need for an autograph in the books. What's up with that?"

"I'm glad you asked, Author." He smiled and pointed to the wall just past where I was seated and continued, "Reach over to the bookshelf to your left and pull down the thick file labeled 'The York Gospel.'"

I paused. "Gospel? Really?"

He sensed my shock and responded with a smirk, "No, don't worry, Author. I've not found religion ... but I did find reality."

He added, "It's called deoxyribonucleic acid—DNA."

"I'm stunned, Doc." It's all I could say.

He opened his file and unpacked something that, as a person of faith, I had never known.

"The York Gospel. It's over a thousand years old ... and, and ..." I stuttered a little bit.

He mercifully interrupted. "It's actually a compilation of the four Gospels—Matthew, Mark, Luke, and John—so it's not an additional Gospel by some Brit named York."

"Right. I get that. And someone was able to do DNA testing on the ancient document—"

He interrupted again, not out of rudeness or frustration but just to keep things accurate. "Sarah Fiddyment."

"What?"

"Not *what*. *Who*. Sarah Fiddyment of York University pioneered the efforts. The one whose paper I asked you to read."

"Oh, um yes, Professor Fiddyment helped develop a technique that used drawing-class erasers for researchers to use by rubbing them on the pages of parchments, creating static electricity and bonding particles together. Am I getting this right?"

He nodded.

"Her team did this to allow bits and pieces of the parchment—and any DNA that would be attached to that parchment—to attach to the eraser particles."

"Right."

"And then those particles were collected and tested for DNA proteins, recovering proteins of both the animal parchment skins and the human authors who wrote on them. Those monks, not the actual original authors, who transcribed the four Gospels."

"It's far more complicated than that, but essentially you're on target." He paused as he finished boiling water for tea. "Science has a way of helping us discover small key aspects of change that, when implemented in life, alter so much. Then, others come along and dial up that change, sometimes in a different direction."

After pouring the piping-hot water into the cup holding his oddly shaped, homemade-looking, silky tea bag, he began stirring the brew with a petite teaspoon and then used the spoon to point to his tea.

"Take, for example, Thomas Sullivan of New York, who saw how this wonderful hot beverage had been served for years. In 1903, a patent was registered for a scientific idea that allowed the tea leaves to be captured in a small satin bag, like the one I'm using. A year later, Sullivan produced his idea commercially.

By 1908—just five years ago, according to where we are in time today—a sort of reverse tea party invasion occurred. The tea invasion of Britain by the Americans occurred. It was successful everywhere."

He smiled, wrapped the string around his tea bag, and squeezed the last little bit of tea into his cup, setting aside the spoon with the spent tea bag in it. Then he took a long sip of tea and placed his cup back on its saucer.

"Umm. So good, though not as good as a coffee from Café Central." He smiled broadly at me and continued.

"A few years after Sullivan, two others from Milwaukee filed for a patent for a 'tea leaf holder' very similar to what we use today. Science in the marketplace."

"Very interesting," I sarcastically said in a low tone.

"Author, you find no connection to tea and the DNA of the York Gospel. Correct?"

Suddenly distracted by my hunger, I nodded casually, looking around for something to eat in his library. "Yeah, exactly." I turned and said, "Hey, I'm starved. Do you have any snacks or crackers around here to go with the tea?"

I stood up, looking around for something, anything. I was famished and more than a little bit bored, I suppose.

"Try the shelf drawer to the left, next to the phonograph," he said, pointing just a dozen steps away from us.

I walked to where the large Edison phonograph was sitting, briefly glanced at his collection of records, and opened the drawer to its left. *Food.*

"A Snickers bar?" I chuckled. "Really? How ... okay, *when* did you bring this back?"

"When we returned from Röhm's America." He paused and then smiled at me. "I figured you might need something when you, umm, *weren't yourself.*"

Unwrapping the candy bar, I took a healthy bite of what some people—not me—consider an unhealthy food. My body reacted like a drunk at a bar downing a shot glass after a long day. I turned toward Doc.

All I said was "Ahhh."

Then I froze.

I turned back to the Edison phonograph with its records loosely scattered around it and immediately grabbed one record.

"Are you kidding me?" I shouted.

Doc knew exactly what I was looking at.

He paused before he responded, "Indeed, it is—since we're speaking of invasions. It's the Beatles."

He smiled his Cheshire Cat smile, "It's the Beatles singing 'I Saw Her Standing There' and 'Money (That's What I Want)' and a few others too. They're all early ones. I liked the early days of the group. I think the latest one I have is 'Yesterday' that Paul McCartney recorded by himself without the band."

I sat looking at this brilliant scientist who suddenly was exposed as fanboy for the Fab Four. With a chuckle, I wondered what could be next.

Summarizing, he said, "I couldn't resist converting some of their music to the vinyl disc that was invented later, *er earlier*, well … you know what I mean."

I couldn't resist, rapidly adding, "And the way it looked was way beyond compare?"

He laughed.

"I liked them as well," I admitted.

"Well, I have all their available autobiographies here for easy reading and enjoy listening to the Beatles from their Hamburg days. What can I say? I'm indeed a fan."

Then he looked at me, as if to move on. I sat down with my Snickers bar nearly finished.

"Author, this is exactly what I'm talking about. Whether its tea bags or LPs, one person invents, another expands, and still another reinvents."

He paused.

"I took the York Gospel technique and expanded it. I created something better."

Nodding, I finished off the candy bar, licking my fingers for any additional stickiness. Then I laughed to myself. *Or for any further DNA.*

Apparently my humor was not transferred to Dr. Gersema through ESP.

He looked at me curiously, wondering what I was laughing about.

"It's nothing; please continue."

He didn't need the invitation to do so. "Every book that's signed by its author contains a trace of his or her DNA near where the signature rests. Every book. I found a way to take the concept of static electricity and magnify it."

"How so?"

"You see, when electricity is at rest, it's referred to as static. It stays and does not move in a current. Electric charges build up on surfaces. They just do. It's the voodoo of science. Static electricity is released when what happens?"

"When friction … or the rubbing of erasers on it occurs, I suppose."

"Well done, Author."

"Yeah, well, thanks. I'm glad it wasn't a calculus question."

He continued. "When the rubbing happens, the atoms of that particular surface lose their electrons, making it now positively charged. The thing that caused the loss is now referred to as negatively charged. Some substances work well together for both the negative and positive charges accepting one another. I learned that human skin and paper/parchments enjoy this mutual acceptance."

"And what about electricity that flows through currents? Wouldn't that burn the paper, let alone the person?"

"Oh, I'm liking this conversation," Doc said, rubbing his hands together.

He stood up and walked to the center of his flat where we had launched ourselves into and out of spacetime.

Spreading his arms out, as would a circus ringleader, he said, "The telluric current—or TC—that runs directly through this library has an otherworldly electrical current that takes the static electricity model and magnifies it to levels far past what will one day be known as regular AC or DC currents. We travel and are not injured, burnt, or harmed."

Then, as if in a mystical trance, he remained standing and closed his eyes. "When we touch our fingers to the DNA surrounding the signature of an author, we are transported via the TC to where and when he signed the book."

"*That's* why we were transported back to my home both times. I wrote my book there."

Opening his eyes and moving toward the bookshelf and phonograph, he leaned against the wall. "Correct."

"So, when I went back to pick up my books, you were looking for the authors who would most help us move through spacetime to end the genocide of the twentieth century."

"Correct again."

"And killing Hitler was not enough."

"We found that out, didn't we? The approach had to be subtler, more selective. And quite honestly, I suppose I had to get the whole 'kill Hitler' thing out of my system, right?"

He added, "We saw what happened as a result."

I shook my head as if revisiting a horrible accident scene and then continued, "I wish we could practice on something before we move forward. Too much hangs in the balance."

Doc paused, as he often did, and smiled. "Maybe this would be the ideal time to invite Lou in to help us, as sort of a practice session?" he asked with a twinkle in his eye. "I want to hold her hand …"

"She better become a fan. That's all I have to say. If she does, that'll make me 'glad all over.'"

Doc just looked at me and slowly deadpanned, "Yeah, yeah, yeah …"

9

1913

The level of Lou Abraham's intelligence was incredible.

We'd hoped for the best and planned for the least when we invited her to Café Central to visit with us again and talk about dimensional travel. The young postgraduate student had no idea what was about to befall her regarding this travel business. The best way Doc felt to tell her was to dig deeper into what she knew of the works of her beloved uncle, Max.

He was sensitive yet direct when the three of us met.

She seemed quite amazed that the previous discussion with Doc and me would bear the type of fruit that this second meeting was now showing. The two of them talked physics, talked Einstein—okay, she yelled a lot during this section—and Doc was gracious as he listened to her family's anecdotal stories about the "theft" of the theory of relativity, bringing her back in line with clearer, more agreeable comments regarding their mutual respect for Isaac Newton.

That's when it got weird. And good.

I said, "Lou, if you could travel through dimensions and correct things so that history as we now know it would change, would you?"

She half closed her eyes, breathed a shallow sort of breath, and then responded, "I would."

Doc then began unveiling all we had been through. His manner was simple and straightforward with a calmness and clarity that surprised me, though I had been his witness to this believably unbelievable journey.

After his presentation was complete, he finished with this invitation: "And we would like you to join us on a small *practice trip*. It'll first involve a little background on music—future music—something that we'll be able to observe as we painlessly experiment. It'll be safe. Are you interested?"

She looked at the two of us with a smirking smile.

Her wide smirk turned to a toothy grin, and that grin was followed by a cackle of pure joy.

"Well, if it's safe, then let's go get as much history as we possibly can. Nothing bad about being a bit piggy here, since pigs get fat ..."

We responded, "And hogs get slaughtered."

Doc motioned to Gunther and Frieda. "Another round of espressos, hot chocolate, and pastries, my friend." Gunther clicked his heels, and his little daughter began collecting cups and plates.

We then began the task of bringing this young postgraduate physics student through the musical wormhole from 1913 to the universe of rock and roll. Her tastes ran to the current songs of "When Irish Eyes Are Shining," "Peg O'My Heart," and "The Spaniard Who Blighted My Life." We were tasked with taking her on a bit of a magical ... mystery tour.

Lou proved more than able for the task—better yet for the *experiment* in spacetime travel—and fairness.

1913, 1959, and 1960

Fairness is an awkward thing. Everyone wants justice for others who offend them and mercy for themselves when they offend others. It's a condition of the human race. As an author, I wrote about that paradigm problem in my first two books—both nonfiction tomes.

And in the end, they didn't sell as well I had hoped. (I suppose that wasn't fair, ha.)

Now, some things *do* sell well. The Beatles sold well.

John, Paul, George, and Ringo burst onto the scene in the early 1960s as Ed Sullivan famously introduced them to millions of Americans on television with what became a famous intro: "Ladies and gentlemen, the Beat-les."

But from 1960 to just before they made their first appearance on English television, they were John, Paul, George, and Pete.

They played together in Liverpool, in Hamburg, eventually on local radio, and in the famed Cavern Club where they were ultimately discovered.

Yet one night while the band was preparing for a set in the Cavern Club, Pete Best—their drummer for roughly two years—came down ill and had to stay home, the legend tells us. The lads were stuck and had to find a substitute band member who played drums. They asked Richey Starkey to sit in.

In time, it was *out* for Pete and *in* for Ringo.

The tale is well known. Pete Best is universally seen as the man who missed stardom by one decision to stay home.

"But what if?" Doc asked Lou and me as he looked over to his easy-reading book area, searching for something. "What if Pete Best had not left the Beatles?"

I looked up. "What?"

"Listen to me, Author. You wanted to see if we could perform a rather harmless experiment before we move into the lives of these evil men at Café Central, right?"

"Yes, that's correct."

"Well, let's right a wrong for one person that might allow us some practice to ensure a successful bigger picture."

"Go on."

He stopped short as he reached up to a higher shelf. "There it is!"

I stood up and walked to where he was, looking at what he now had in his hand. He held a book and two drumsticks, both of which had an autograph and a date. One read "Pete Best, 1959" in black marker ink. The other was similar, only with 1960 on it.

"These drumsticks took me a while to obtain. The book I bought on Amazon, it's called *Beatle! The Pete Best Story* and … bingo!"

"Don't you mean Ringo?"

"What?" he said as he turned toward me, flipping the pages at the front of the book.

"Nothing," I said, having lost the moment.

Lou looked at both of us, somewhat lost.

"All right, Author, let's have some fun with history. Are you ready?"

Only one expression came to mind in response. "Rock 'n' roll."

Doc, Lou, and I placed our thumbs on the autograph of Pete Best, on the 1959 drumstick, stepped onto TC1, closed our eyes, holding the book, and in a fraction of a moment were gone.

As we opened our eyes, a very different world met us.

It was the world of Liverpool, England, in 1959.

Though looking almost ancient to our present-day lifestyles and customs, this version of Liverpool was actually in Lou's future. She stood silent and breathless, slowly taking it all in.

To be honest, I'd always wanted to visit Liverpool, if only to see where the Beatles came from. My partner in spacetime travel, however, was *giddy* as we stepped away from the TC in the downtown area.

"Hahaha, we're in Liverpool, mate!" Doc said with unabashed joy as we walked down Falkner Street.

"*Mate?* isn't that a bit Aussie for us to use here in Liverpool?"

"Well, not really. Liverpool at one time was the emigration station for the UK. Many citizens left for Australia. They gave the Aussies the word mate, *mate*," he said with far too big of a smile as we began our walking tour away from the surprisingly large downtown area. He was just beside himself with giddiness.

Opening up Best's autobiography, Doc reviewed his notes in the back of the book and began reading his own notes on the back page of the paperback copy. He walked as he read.

"They had emigrants and immigrants exiting and entering Liverpool for many years. In fact, Pete Best's mom was originally from India. Pete was born there. She married his dad, who was a British subject and moved to Liverpool when Pete and his brother, Rory, were just kids."

His stride was increasingly matching his level of excitement. As we walked a long distance, Doc occasionally looked at his copy of Best's book. Lou just seemed to tag along like a lost puppy.

Approaching a beautiful Victorian residential structure, he announced, "Here we are, 8 Haymans Green."

"And?"

We paused.

"It's Pete's home, actually his mom's home. She bought it after reportedly winning a horse race where the odds were thirty-three to one. The name of the winning horse seemed quite appropriate for the entire Best family: Never Say Die. She actually built a band area and coffee shop inside the residence and called it the Casbah Coffee Club." He smiled the smile of a fan about to meet a hero.

"It's the first public place that John, Paul, and George played and were paid for doing so. And we're going to go into the coffee shop for coffee."

"Do they serve hot chocolate?" I said, without any intention of being answered.

The Casbah was well lit and full of fun. Young people in their 1950s apparel were everywhere—dancing, drinking sodas, and talking at small tables. Just as happened in Vienna, we saw our clothes change when we arrived downtown. Since we were not teens, our conservative sport coats and simple shirts blended in with the crowd of chaperones standing along the outside.

I picked up a discarded copy of the *Mersey Beat* news magazine. The date said December 1959.

Doc and I scanned the audience. Two teenage brothers were helping a middle-aged lady clean tables and bus empty glasses and dishes.

Doc took an educated guess as to who the two teenage boys were.

"Hey, Pete, come over here," he said with authority.

The taller of the two boys threw his damp rag over his left shoulder, adjusted his half apron, and walked over.

"How can I help you?" he asked. "Do I know you? How'd you know my name?"

"Oh, I know of Mona's success at the races and just took a wild guess that you were her oldest."

"That I am," he said with a thick Liverpool accent and a wide grin.

"Do you have a moment?" Doc asked.

"Sure, let me tell my kid brother to take over for me." He turned to his brother and yelled, "Go on with yourself, mate. Finish my job," throwing his wadded-up wet towel across the small room, over the heads of the teens. Both brothers' smiles spoke loudly of their love for each other.

We all sat down together.

Pete nodded to Lou, smiled, and said, "You seem a bit older than the teens who show up here. When were you born?"

"Eighteen ninety-one," she responded, without blinking an eye.

Pete looked at all of us, then laughed. "Well, I don't detect a Liverpool accent, but I do detect that you're a bit daft like the rest of us! Welcome to the Casbah ..."

"Lou," she said.

"What's that short for? Louise?"

She blushed and nodded.

Doc and I found out something new about our graduate student from 1913.

"Who's he?" Pete asked, pointing at me.

Not knowing what else to say, I said, "I'm with him," pointing to Doc.

"And you're all three from the States, according to your accents. Want a Coke?"

We obliged, and he lovingly insulted his younger brother again.

"Get four Cokes, and if you see Mo, have her stop by. We've got us some regular Yanks in the Casbah today!" He nodded in our direction to his brother.

Lou asked, "Are Cokes still only a nickel?" to everyone's surprise. After a quick currency conversion, Pete Best looked up and said, "Yes, they are, Miss Louise." Then he turned to Doc and me.

"Okay, what can I do for you?"

We both paused and looked at each other, realizing that we hadn't thought through what we'd say to Pete Best.

As always, Doc was quicker than I.

"Well, we understand that you have bands playing here on a regular basis."

"That we do."

"And we also understand that you have a band yourself. My guess is you play here as well as do dishes, right?"

He laughed. "With Mona, of course I *have* to do both."

Just as he was speaking, a voice came from behind.

"What's my boy laughing at now?"

We turned to see Mona Best, a nice-looking woman in her midforties, approach us with a tray and three bottles of Coca-Cola with straws in them.

"Hello. I heard over the crowd noise that you three are from America." Pete shot Rory a wink across the floor as their mother pulled up a chair in a welcoming family sort of way.

Doc opened the discussion. "Mrs. Best, we—"

"Call me Mona, for goodness' sakes. Even my boys call me Mo."

"Okay, Mona." Pointing to me, he said, "This is Peter Frampton, and I'm Willie Nelson. And this is uh, um …"

Pete interrupted. "This is Miss Louise, Mum."

Mona nodded, taking inventory of this young lady as only a middle-aged woman can.

Doc continued, "And we're in the music business in the US. We understand that your son plays drums with local bands. Is that right?"

"Indeed he does, Mr. Nelson."

"Please call me Willie."

She nodded.

We both took large gulps from our very small 1950s Coke bottles. Lou seemed to enjoy this common bubbly taste sensation from her childhood. And like a child in a fantasy, she was trying to connect with a world so different from her own yet with strands of similarity.

"Doesn't the cocaine taste great in this?" she innocently asked while wiping off the fizzy residue from her lips with her free hand.

Mona smiled. "Yes, but they're taking it out starting next year, lass," she said, as though it was just simple, direct truth, understood by all.

Not missing a beat, Doc turned and continued, "And we think that your son ought to consider going over to Hamburg, Germany, for some extensive playing. Our record label sends scouts to Hamburg on a regular basis to see the hot, new talent."

"Your record label?" Mona said with a crescendo of interest in her voice. "What's it called?"

Doc seemed stymied, as though caught in a logical conundrum of what to say next.

I spoke up. "It's called Apple. Steve Jobs started it a while back." I took another chug of the Coca-Cola, neither of us looking at the other, fearful that one of us would blow residual cola out of our noses in laughter.

"Oh, it sounds so American …"

"Mr. Frampton and I think Pete might just catch on. He sings as well as play drums, correct?"

"Like a lark, he does," his proud mama said as he sat next to her, blushing.

"Well, think about it, and, Pete, be open to heading to Hamburg," he said.

Pete nodded obediently, like any starstruck fifteen-year-old musician would.

"My talent agents, or maybe even Mr. Frampton and I, will look forward to connecting in Hamburg. We've got to leave now," Doc finished abruptly as we stood up to leave.

Mona spoke up as though she was about to lose her son's single chance at stardom. "How would Pete meet you there?"

"Oh, just have him stop by the Kaiserkeller. Someone will be there for him."

As we walked out of the Casbah, I realized that Doc was about to change the lives of Pete and Ringo, but I was wrong by 50 percent.

I later learned it went something like this: The week before John, Paul, George, and Stuart Sutcliffe—wearing his now-signature sunglasses—were to head to Hamburg, they needed a drummer. It was August 12, 1960, and they were scheduled to be on stage in six days. Pete and Mona had given the lads a lot of exposure in Liverpool, so their relationship was quite warm. As history tells the story, Pete had a drum set, so he was asked to be in the band. He jumped at the chance. Less than a week later, he was performing as a Beatle. They played many Hamburg venues and grew stronger as musicians.

By December 1960, George Harrison was sent back to England for being underage, McCartney and Best were deported for one reason or another, Lennon returned by his own volition, and Sutcliffe stayed in Hamburg with a newly acquired German girlfriend.

The band reunited and returned to Hamburg not too much later in the spring of 1961. Sutcliffe soon left the Beatles, deciding that art was his real love. One year later, he died of a cerebral hemorrhage, suffered as a result of a bar fight when he was a Beatle.

By November 1962, they returned a third time to Hamburg to play another set of clubs, only this time Ringo was playing drums, Pete was fired by a combination of bandmates and managers, and Stuart was dead.

That's what happened in history. Pete Best missed being a member of the internationally known Fab Four by just months.

What was about to happen in this new history was surprising and showed a little deeper understanding of Doc's sense of fairness and subtlety.

The rhyme scheme of rock 'n' roll history was about to change. We exchanged the first drumstick for the one dated 1960. It did its magic.

In December 1960, Peter Frampton, Willie Nelson, and Miss Louise arrived in Hamburg. Stuart Sutcliffe was still alive, and the Beatles had five members.

Walking into the Kaiserkeller, Pete Best saw us before we saw him.

Turning toward the small group of people near him, he said, "Lads, here are the two record producers from America I told you about! Well, it's about time."

The group turned toward us. There in front of us were *very* young versions of John Lennon, Paul McCartney, and George

Harrison. Stuart Sutcliffe was with them as well, yet I didn't notice the eternally young version of him. He wasn't wearing his sunglasses.

We pulled up chairs around a small table, and John ordered the table a round of scotch and Cokes.

"So what's the deal, Mr. Hollywood record producer? Are you serious about looking for an English band in Hamburg?" John asked.

"We are."

George said, "Why us?"

I couldn't help but weigh in. "You might not be the ones we want. We'll give a listen and tell you. We like Pete and his style. We also love his mother."

"Who doesn't love Mona?" George responded.

The waitress brought eight scotch and Cokes, and John reached for his wallet.

"I'll take care of the tab, boys," I said with as much bravado as I thought a Hollywood record producer would have.

"If you're for real," said Paul. The others seemed embarrassed by his quick cut.

I pulled out my wallet, suddenly realizing that all I had was an American Express card and it most likely had not been invented yet. Doc saw the fear glance across my eyes and distracted the group from this reaction.

"Well done, Mr. Frampton. Hasn't it been nice to have the American Express since '58? You boys have an American Express card, don't you?"

They looked at the ground, a couple scuffing the soles of their shoes against the table, embarrassed.

I nodded, handing over the card to the waitress, and the Beatles sat amazed that a piece of plastic, a simple card with numbers on it, could pay for something.

Pete piped in. "I told you they were from Hollywood, lads. They're from our future!"

Doc and I both decided not to look at each other or respond to that odd comment.

"We're a good band. I even play drums when I'm needed," said Paul. It seemed to me he was trying to bring a sense of camaraderie back to this drinking session.

Doc nodded. "Well, with Pete's skill and his nice drum set, you won't be needed as a drummer, right?"

"Of course not. I'm just very versatile. That's all I was trying to say," responded Paul.

I couldn't help but release a small chuckle.

He responded defensively, "I *am*. I'm very good. My dad's a musician and has taught me a lot."

"Oh, I don't doubt it. I'll just … let it be at that." I looked over at Doc, and he rolled his eyes.

Pete said, "We're on stage in three minutes, lads. We need to get ready."

The most prolific band in modern music was about to audition for the two phoniest record producers in history.

I smiled and took a large sip of scotch and Coke. "I think I need this," I said to Doc.

10

1960 and 1961

When the twenty-five-minute set was over, Doc, Lou, and I had heard so many tunes in their infancy: "The Pinwheel Twist," "Money (That's What I Want)," "I Saw Her Standing There," "My Bonnie," and even an early version of something that sounded remarkably like "Love Me Do," though it did not have those lyrics.

When the boys were on the stage, they looked raw. They had threadbare suits and skinny ties, like every other musical act of 1961. They wanted to look professional but simply didn't. Soon enough, they'd replace those cheap suits with leather jackets and jeans. By 1964, they'd be back in matching English suits.

Their break came, and they rejoined us for another round of drinks. This time, George ordered. "Let's have something much different, lads. Umm, let's see." He folded his chin into his clenched fist in a mocking impression of deep thought. "Let's have rum ... and scotch ... and Coke."

"Here, here!" the band responded.

Pete Best then asked Stuart Sutcliffe if he had anything to say.

"Well, not really but maybe." He looked directly into my eyes and asked if I'd ever been in a fight.

"A fistfight?"

"Or with beer bottles, I suppose."

"In school I did."

John said, "They let you drink beer in American high schools?" We all laughed.

"And you, Stuart? Do fights find you?" Doc asked.

"Last week, one did—right outside this club. Outside, I was slammed right up against the Kaiserkeller's brick wall, and a barmy man started a fight with me. He slammed me good into that wall. My head felt like it cracked in the back. The boys dragged me out of there and saved my life."

John added, "I broke me finger. Paul, remember?"

"I was gone to meet a bird," Paul responded.

I replied with a question to Stuart, "Why did you ask me that?"

"Well, Mr. Frampton, we're mates, and we stay together."

John suddenly added with a lilt in his voice, "Unless of course one of us wants out."

I nodded, finishing my scotch and Coke as my new drink of rum and scotch and Coke showed up. Lou seemed contented just having her refill be a Coke.

I liked Stuart Sutcliffe. I was starting to like the Beatles' drinks too.

The walk back to their sleeping quarters was a jovial time filled with humor. I noticed that Pete and Stuart were having a deep discussion. I joined them. Doc stayed walking with John, George, and Paul.

I waited for an opening and then said plainly to Stuart, "I'll take you in the morning to the doctor to have your head x-rayed."

He was taken aback by my boldness.

"I know of a man in history who had exactly what you had happen, and it remained unchecked for far too long. He ultimately died from it because he never had it examined." I paused and then said for effect, "He was an artist."

Stuart saw that I cared. He stood still, forcing half of us to stand still with him.

"Okay, mate. I'll go with you in the morning. Thank you." Then we all walked into the night.

The next day allowed Doc and me to meet Stuart at a local Hamburg hospital, and the results of the x-ray showed what two of the three of us already knew. It was a severe skull fracture, and Stuart was immediately hospitalized. There was also present a small tumor, which was removed.

We sat with him in his hospital room as he recuperated and got to know him. In Beatle folklore, this attractive twenty-year-old was the "unknown Beatle" who prematurely left the most famous rock 'n' roll group in history and tragically died. He was a sort of cold and distant second-string James Dean / Marilyn Monroe black-and-white photographic image.

Yet, the alive version of Stu, as he asked us to call him, was a warm and sensitive artist who only played bass with this particular group so that he could have money to live in Germany and paint. He was enrolled in the Hamburg College of Art, and he loved his fiancée, Astrid. Life was good.

Until it wasn't. And then again, until it was; 1960 became 1961.

And now this version of Stu Sutcliffe was being healed. Each day as we visited him, the medical doctors administered a collection of medications, including painkillers, diuretics, steroids, and anticonvulsants.

And each day, two or three of the four other bandmates visited him. Absent, often for good reasons, was Paul. He was getting gigs for the group but didn't let them know.

Stu took notice of his absence.

It was during that week that Doc talked plainly with Stu about the need for him to ensure that Pete Best stay a part of the Beatles.

"What are ya, daft?" Stu at first responded. "I'm the one supposedly with a tumor and a head injury." He paused, and we laughed. "Of course Pete's gonna stay. Why would he not? We started in his house, and Mona was so kind to us."

Doc knowingly looked at me and then looked back at Stu.

"Stu, I want you to promise me a couple of things."

"Anything, Willie."

I chuckled to myself as I heard his sincerity mixing with the famous name Doc had used for himself.

"I know you're thinking of leaving the band."

Stu looked as though Doc had been reading his mail.

"Before you leave the band, I want you to teach Pete to play bass, moving Paul to drums ... since he loves playing drums anyway. You're the band's unofficial creative leader, and because of that, I want you to use your newfound good health to help all of them as you exit."

Stu looked amazed at us. "I actually had been thinking of changing things up a bit, but me headaches from me split skull stopped it cold."

He looked out the window. Then he said something rather vulnerable.

"I think Pete could learn the bass quickly. I certainly did. In a way, I wonder if it's just not time for Paul to go solo ... to go his own way. He's so terrifically talented."

Stu continued, "I know a drummer that could fill the empty slot. His name's Richie Starkey. He's from Liverpool too."

Doc and I both looked ahead. The wheels were in motion.

It was time for us to leave.

Before we did, I asked Stu to do something for himself.

"Okay, what?"

"When you formally leave the Beatles as a musician, I want you to remain on as a 20 percent owner of the band, doing artwork for their albums."

"Albums? What albums?"

"Don't worry; there'll be albums," Doc said matter-of-factly.

"And even if we, at Apple, end up not being your record producers, make sure that every original song that is written has an equal split for all five of you, given that you bring Ringo in."

"How'd you know we call him Ringo? Did you see a poster of him and the band the Hurricanes?"

I smiled. "Might have." Then I lowered my tone. "And give equal credit to all the songs as Lennon-Harrison-Sutcliffe-Best-Starkey."

"That's a fairly big mouthful and a bit awkward," he said.

"Fairness can be awkward sometimes," Doc said.

Lou saw what was happening and entered into the spirit of the conversation. "May I ask a favor?"

Stu smiled and said, "Of course!"

"Would you name a song for me?"

Stu sat up in his hospital bed, put on his signature sunglasses, and smiled. "Well, I'm not that much of a songwriter." He paused, looked intently at Louise. "But John and George just wrote an instrumental tune called 'Cry for a Shadow.' Maybe I'll ask them to rename it for you."

Doc looked up and whispered, "That would be nice indeed; no more possibility of *crying*."

We each hugged Stu and turned to leave.

As the three of us exited his hospital room, we heard him say through a smile, "Thanks, mates, for saving my life."

The three of us smiled. Our practice run was completed.

1913

Returning to January 1913 in Vienna had now become normal for us. It's an odd thing to even say.

In our recent approach, we'd observed that dimensional travel could work tactically, changing things that we felt needed to be changed with relatively minor alterations to the fabric of time and space.

And, conveniently enough, without inciting the deaths of millions of people.

Our first attempt at changing the world through killing Hitler was unsuccessful. This most recent gentle spacetime journey to Liverpool worked well. We even saved a life, changed the future, and felt good about it. Now, we needed to think strategically, globally.

So, here we were, back where we'd begun. And yet we were deeply changed. Having Lou with us was such a beneficial addition; her presence added joy to our band. Deep, true joy.

Sitting in the library, we again took the measure of one another and the place in spacetime where we now found ourselves.

"The fact remains, Author, that we must use the skills we developed in Liverpool to stop the pending carnage soon to be perpetrated by those nefarious despots-in-the-making at Café Central, just blocks away from us. To do that, we must look differently at the same set of facts."

"How so?"

"Well, let's think back." He took a long drink of water from the crystal tumbler that previously (and regularly) held his liquor.

"Let's place all facts before us. We've simply been looking at them in a way that hasn't worked—like a man with an incorrect eyeglass prescription. It's cloudy and fuzzy and doesn't make sense, but the lack of clarity doesn't cover up what's really real. There's something we're missing. We need new glasses."

"I agree," I said, squinting my eyes in hope that some type of brain exercises might kick into gear and help me think differently.

"What are you doing?" he asked me. "You look like *you* need new glasses."

"I'm doubling down."

"What?"

"I'm doubling down—as a gambler does—putting more energy into my thinking. The squinting is just how it registers on my face," I said, embarrassed somewhat by being caught in the act of this childhood behavior that I've used over the years.

"You look like a bad impersonation of Liam Neeson on a bad day," he said, laughing.

"No, I don't," I said, laughing back at him. Turning to Lou, I added, "He's a film star in the future, even bigger than Douglas Fairbanks."

"Impossible," she gushed. "Douglas Fairbanks is every woman's beau ideal."

"And Liam Neeson is everyone's idea of what a regular guy should be," I said, a bit too testy, I realized.

Doc avoided the internecine squabble. "Well, I suppose if it works for you, go ahead and squint away, Liam. I just hope you don't end up in one of our spacetime dimensions with somebody being taken."

I laughed. It was needed at the moment.

"Hey, I noticed that you're enjoying water now and not alcohol. Earlier, when you poured the contents of that tumbler down the drain, you said it was for clarity on our project. Is something else going on?"

He looked at me, and a small smirk replaced his broad smile.

"Clarity in life, I suppose." He nodded as if that was all that was needed and folded his hands, again in thought. "Now let's focus—or squint, if you will—on the clarity needed for this situation."

Lou added, "Well, you could always let cocaine soothe you while you drink a Coca-Cola."

I laughed. Lou looked totally embarrassed. Doc became instantly kind to Lou in his expression. He then took a few minutes to describe how Coke no longer had any trace of coke in it. The discussion was needful if only to avoid awkward moments in the future between Lou and others we might encounter. She soon understood the nuances of the discussion and agreed not to bring it up again.

We sat in three comfortable chairs in the library of the flat. Dr. Russell Gersema eventually closed his eyes, as he so often did, and silence fell on us for many minutes.

I sat squinting.

He sat thinking.

Lou sat learning, reading portions of books from Doc's library.

Soon, in a very low, modulated voice, he began recalling the facts. "We know that in 1913, Hitler was a simple young man with complex personal problems who failed as an artist here in Vienna, early in his life. From that failure, coupled with his need to be accepted, he gravitated in time from art to social activism. In time, his hatred for Jews became his terrible guiding light."

He breathed deeply and continued, "And we know that Putzi Hanfstaengl was a mentor to him soon after Hitler joined the Nazi Party."

"What we don't know is whether Putzi had a corresponding hatred for Jews, which fed into Hitler," I said. "They could have gotten together strictly out of friendship of sorts."

Doc reached for a white notebook of loose-leaf papers and his fountain pen and took notes as we spoke.

"And we know that Putzi's mother was American, and his father was a wealthy German publisher. There was a reason he went to Harvard. My guess is that his parents wanted him to see the world through the lens of American capitalism and political thought."

I interjected, "Or maybe just to be close to their wealthy New York lifestyle?"

"That could be," Doc responded. "And maybe both reasons did combine to allow a young Berliner to move to Boston."

He wrote some more down and then pointed to my books on his side table.

"Author, open up U. S. Grant's memoirs and turn to the section where Grant writes of General John Sedgwick's death during the Civil War in 1864."

"Putzi's relative?"

"Yes. When you find it, please read it to me. John Sedgwick was a unique man, beloved by his superior officers as well as by his troops. The common infantry soldier referred to him as Uncle John. That's a rarity in the US Army, both then and now."

I only half listened because I was focused. Having tabbed it before, I found the section he requested.

"It's in chapter 52 and reads as follows: 'By noon of the 9th (of May 1864) the position of the two armies was as follows: Lee occupied a semicircle facing north, north-west and north-east, enclosing the town. Anderson was on his left extending to the Po River, Warren occupied our right, covering the Brock and other roads converging at Spottsylvania; Sedgwick was to his left and Burnside on our extreme left.

"'In the morning General Sedgwick was killed near the right of his entrenchments by rebel sharpshooters. His loss was a severe one to the Army of the Potomac and to the Nation.'"

I closed volume 2 of what most historians say is the best memoir by any former president of the United States.

Doc said, "A simple yet profound statement, 'His loss was a severe one to the Army of the Potomac and to the Nation.' Eyewitnesses spoke of Grant's reactions when he received word of General John Sedgwick's death at the hands of a sharpshooter. 'Is he really dead?' he asked through tears, as he fell backward into a hard wooden chair. Grant later said that Sedgwick's death was 'greater than the loss of a whole division of troops.'" Doc paused. "That's equal to up to fifteen thousand men. Extraordinary."

Lou and I watched Doc, deep in thought.

Doc continued, "We also know that Orrin Backus served with General Grant and owned a signed copy of the memoirs. Both Backus and Grant signed volume 1 of the two-volume set. We have one copy here with us, the one you retrieved on your first spacetime journey."

He continued, "This second volume may actually be quite useful to us after all." He clapped his hands and sat up straight, as if being a student called on in class to recite an answer he fully knew. He retrieved the copy of Grant's memoir and began leafing through the pages, scanning them for something.

"Doc, what are you doing?"

"Shhh, let me look."

Page after page was turned, increasing in rapidity.

Finally, midway through the roughly 650 pages of volume 2, he stopped, read a page, and then looked directly at me.

"Author, you, Lou, and I may have a way to change one more person's life and therefore change time."

1913

The idea was smart and subtle. Doc laid out the plan with a quiet, logical force that drew us in.

"So you're saying that General John Sedgwick's death by a Confederate sharpshooter in May 1864 could have—"

"Does have," Doc said, interrupting.

"Okay, *does have* a direct impact on both the duration of the Civil War and how Putzi Hanfstaengl's life turned out, thus influencing Adolf Hitler's life?"

"Correct. Putzi's grandmother was born a Sedgwick and was the general's cousin. His grandfather was another Union Civil War general, William Heine. The death of John Sedgwick was so profound to not just General Grant but to the whole nation. His loss convulsed the Union cause, and many believe that the Civil War was extended another year because Grant's right-hand man was killed by a sniper.

"Not many know of him, unless you're a deep-dive history buff like me or attended West Point ... like you."

"Ha, I didn't realize you'd done a deep-dive history search on me!"

"Indeed, Author. Though not a graduate, you spent two of your undergraduate years at West Point, where you developed your distaste for calculus. Correct?"

"Let's just say that the dean did not have much of a tolerance for my propensity for low math grades," I said as I chuckled.

"And Sedgwick was part of your life at West Point, wasn't he?"

"You mean because of his statue with the spurs that spun?" I responded.

"You knew that statue well, didn't you, Author?"

I did.

Lou said, "Please explain the statue comment."

"In West Point lore, any West Point cadet deficient in a subject can, at the stroke of midnight the night before a major test, spin the moveable spurs on the boot heels of General John Sedgwick's statue, and the general's luck would help that cadet pass his (and later, her) final exam the next morning.

"Let's just say that in my two years at West Point, my fingertips left enough traces of DNA to force a guilty plea for having more fun at the academy than study time.

"I never did understand why a general who was shot through the head by a sniper as he stood up in battle and with his last words stated, 'They couldn't hit an elephant at this distance,' would become the symbol for good luck at the world's premier military academy."

Macabre as it was, we still laughed.

Then Doc caught himself and stopped. "And yet, if I *am* correct, his death altered his family's line and changed things at a root level, regarding the length of the Civil War."

"Doc, fill me in regarding the specifics of what we do now."

"Since Orrin Backus wrote in the section that describes Sedgwick's death, and his DNA is on that page because of his writing, it'll allow one of us to head directly to where Backus was on the battlefield. It'll be an interesting introduction."

I said, "I'll use Putzi's book—the pages where he comments also about the death of Sedgwick. His DNA will allow me to approach the general and stop him from standing up. It might have to happen through force.

"Wow, tackling a commanding general of tens of thousands of loyal soldiers in the very midst of a Civil War battle. It'll be a suicide mission."

"No, Author, it'll be a wrestling match. No guard will draw his weapon and fire on a rolling mass of humanity that includes a major general."

"Anything else?" I asked.

Lou asked, "What should I do while the two of you head back to the 1860s?"

Doc answered in a kind and directed fashion, "Lou, I want you to study Brian Greene's work in *The Elegant Universe*. It will stretch you, especially when he talks about Albert Einstein."

She couldn't resist. "Don't you men Albert I-stole-it?"

"Well, read and learn. Dr. Greene's work is phenomenal and will blow your mind."

Lou looked sheepish and suddenly scared. "Why would I want my mind to be exploded? That would be terrible. I would die."

I interrupted this cross-dimensional, cross-cultural linguistic conflict. "It's a figure of speech that means you will learn much more than you can believe right now."

Doc kept his glance on me, expecting an answer to *his* question.

"I wish I could add more. I think though that we need to just get to Spotsylvania Court House on May 9, 1864, and quickly interject ourselves at the moment described by Putzi in his book and explained by Grant in his."

He gathered up both books, handing Putzi's book to me and holding onto Grant's book himself. "Author, we'll be traveling to the same place at the same time, though we'll be in two different areas of the battlefield. Our job is to stop General Sedgwick from being shot. I'll introduce myself to Orrin Backus, who will be shuttling soldiers across the Po River, and we'll take out the sniper. You tackle the general." He paused. "You wrestled at West Point, didn't you?"

We both laughed, and I said, "Yeah, but his weight class might be a little bit heavier than mine, with all those general's stars on his shoulders."

Doc looked at me and matter-of-factly said, "Whatever you do, win this match."

Simultaneously, we opened the two books, placed our thumbs on the DNA areas, and were gone.

1864

I can't vouch for Doc's arrival, but mine was relatively peaceful and therefore quite disconcerting, since we were supposed to be in a battle. I expected huge cannonade crashes and Rebel yells. This was, after all, the Battle of Spotsylvania Court House where over thirty-two thousand men fell.

It was quiet. Almost deadly so.

I arrived at the intersection where the two branches of Brock Road met and heard men whistling. I saw men moving awkwardly, almost as if they were dancing this way and that as they walked and whistled.

It was strange sort of sporadic whistle, like you might employ to catch the attention of a child or a dog—a sort of one-note wonder. The strange thing was that the men's whistles were uniform, almost identical.

A thought hit me as I closed in on the commanding officers assembled near the edge of Brock Road. Was their music so monotone in the 1860s that these soldiers just whistled one note repeatedly? Since we changed the Beatles in the 1960s, maybe we could improve music for these guys in the 1860s.

That thought was quickly interrupted.

As I stood next to one of the many oak trees overhanging the road, I watched, trying to spot Major General John Sedgwick. I saw a general officer approach a young enlisted man, so I moved closer, being able to do so since I was now clothed in a Union uniform, that of a junior grade officer.

I could barely make out what he said, so I pressed in closer, listening to the enlisted man whistle as he dodged to the ground and they talked. The general tapped him gently with his foot as the enlisted man lay on the ground. He seemed to be a man of great mirth and joy.

"Why, my man, I am ashamed of you, dodging that way. They couldn't hit an elephant at this distance."

I suddenly realized that the whistles weren't whistles. They were rounds fired from Rebel snipers, passing by each of us, leaving one-note whistling sounds as they did so. Men weren't whistling and dancing. They were dodging death, one awkward leap at a time.

The general officer kept talking to the enlisted man, who at this point stood and dusted himself off from the dirt. The young man saluted the general.

I also stood up ramrod straight, slightly behind the oak tree, and said out loud to myself, "That's Sedgwick. That's the last thing he said before he was shot." I had this miserable feeling that his end would happen before I could throw him to the dusty ground.

Yet it wasn't the last thing that he said. History was only partially accurate, it turned out.

I left the safety of the tree and advanced quickly in hopes of saving him. No round hit him.

The enlisted man kept talking as I closed in, increasing my pace.

He said, "General, I dodged a shell once. I believe in dodging."

The general laughed and replied, "All right, my man, go to your place."

He turned to his aide-de-camp and began to repeat the same sentence, "Why, they couldn't hit an elephant ..."

Oh my God, I thought and acted immediately. I lunged at the general and tackled him to the ground, his aide-de-camp and the enlisted man standing in shock as I did so.

Sedgwick's body bounced off of the ground and then off of me as we rolled to a stop. His eyes were wide as saucers as he exchanged glances between his aide and me.

At that very moment, the killer round whistled by the aide's right ear, jamming itself into that midsized oak treat against which I had just seconds ago been leaning. He and the enlisted man fell to the ground, joining the general and myself.

"What in tarnation did you do, my man?" General John Sedgwick said as he disentangled himself from my grasp and used his hat to dust off his uniform. He regained his footing and stood up with help from his aide and the enlisted man.

Before I could respond, the aide-de-camp looked directly at the general and said, "General, this officer saved your life."

"He sure did, General," said the enlisted man. "He made a *dodger* out of you before you even knew it, by golly."

General John Sedgwick looked at all three of the men surrounding him and then smiled the type of smile that obviously endeared him to his troops. "Well, I guess Uncle John is still alive to help win this war," he said, reaching out to shake my hand.

"And your name is?"

Somehow it just came out of my mouth, "General, I'm Tommy Lasorda."

"Italian, heh? Well, Lasorda, you made both of us dodgers today."

I smiled the smile of every Los Angeles baseball fan.

He turned and strode off with his aide.

My trip was a little bit shorter, moving back toward the oak tree and then turning left at Vienna.

11

1913

I returned to our flat in Vienna sooner than Dr. Gersema. Lou was curled up reading on the large sofa chair, about three-quarters through Brian Greene's book. She noticed me only because she stopped for a drink of water. Apparently, Doc hadn't filled up his icebox with Coca-Cola as he normally did.

"This book is extraordinary. My uncle Max would absolutely love it. I certainly do." Then she dove back into the book, and I realized that she was not talking to me, just talking out loud for her own benefit and processing.

Arriving early also gave me the unique opportunity to see exactly what others would see as eyewitnesses to our arrivals from different spacetime dimensions.

The light surrounding Doc's reentry to our flat was unexpected, especially since there was no accompanying heat. It was more like an actor slipping out from behind a curtain onto a stage and then met by the brilliant limelight of calcium oxide flames with an intense glow but no heat. Brilliant and then gone. No wonder I wasn't noticed on a battlefield.

Doc stepped from the TC to the center of the flat. He was not alone.

My partner in dimensional spacetime travel casually looked at me as though introducing a new friend at a dinner party.

"Author, may I introduce Captain Orrin Backus to you and Lou. And, Captain, these are my partners in all that I described to you, Lou and Author."

Riverboat captain Orrin Backus, the original owner of my copy of Grant's memoirs, stood directly in front of me.

However surprised I was, he had the look of a puppy just born into the world—as Louise had when she first traveled with us.

"This is extraordinary," he gulped as he steadied himself, grabbing hold of the back of a chair, eventually turning to sit down in it.

"I am in Vienna, Austria?" he asked, turning to Dr. Gersema. Doc nodded. "In January 1913."

Then Doc turned to us. "Author and Lou, when he has recovered, Mr. Backus has much to tell us about which we previously knew very little."

I furrowed my brow in interest and leaned toward him. Lou joined me. Orrin Backus simply sat down next to Lou, stunned, looking around the library. He appeared shell-shocked.

In a bit of a hushed tone, I put it straight to the doctor. "What were you thinking bringing a stranger into this already confusing and potentially lethal world of dimensional spacetime travel?"

"I had to. Please allow me to explain. And he's not a stranger. He loaned you his Grant book, didn't he?" he asked through a smirk.

I inclined my ear to hear him quietly speak but wouldn't yet let him have the final word on the conversation. "I *bought* those books from his estate. Or I should say that my wife did."

He shrugged and changed the subject, smiling. "Well done in rescuing General Sedgwick from the head wound. I could see your actions through field glasses."

I nodded as though this type of conversation had become quite normal now.

He continued, "I landed near Mr. Backus's two riverboat ships on the Po River near the battlefield. As I anticipated, they were being used to transport Union troops across the river to set up the attack. I looked for Captain Backus and upon finding him began to explain my need to disrupt the Confederate snipers' nest, full of Whitworth rifles—the nest from which the fatal shot would have been delivered to General Sedgwick. I needed a Union sharpshooter. I also needed a high vantage point from which to gain a clear field of fire. Captain Backus provided both for me without questioning my credentials or my rank."

"Uh huh," I said, wondering how Doc had managed to translate these actions into an invitation to the future for the riverboat captain.

"And he joined me with the sharpshooter—a young man from Connecticut—when I pointed out to them where the hive of snipers was."

Doc pointed to the swooning couch and had us both sit down on it.

"While the sharpshooter peppered the Rebel snipers' nest, I watched through my field glasses. The young Connecticut soldier was focused yet a bit chatty."

"I guess so."

"What do you mean?"

"Well, as you two sat chatting away, those Rebel sharpshooters kept whistling Dixie through their Whitworth rifles at the general, his camp, and at me!"

"They weren't sharpshooters; they were snipers," he said, correcting me. "Only the Union carried Sharps rifles, so only the Union could field riflemen called sharpshooters."

Sometimes Doc's attention to details was so irritating to me, especially when it was followed up by his all-knowing smirk, which was the case here.

"You err, Author. The Connecticut Yankee on Captain Backus's boat had seven kills. All snipers were eliminated in that hive."

"And yet the round that should have killed Sedgwick still made its way to the Union camp, lodging itself in a tree trunk."

"It was a stray round," the riverboat captain said as he slowly stood up and approached us. "It had to be a stray round and not from a sniper. The general's elephant comment that you told me about, Professor, was correct. The Whitworth rifle could not have made a surgical strike on the Union camp from the distance of that nest. The Sharps could though, and that was to those seven men's eternal undoing."

Backus seemed to have recovered his faculties.

Doc and I stood up from the swooning couch.

"Professor?" I said under my breath to Doc.

"He started calling me that when I told him I wasn't a medical doctor," he mumbled.

"Captain, please tell us what you make of your traveling through space and time," Doc said.

Orrin Backus looked at both of us in a curious, wide-eyed way, as though we were from another world. *Wait. We sort of are,* I thought to myself.

He turned to me, "May I call you Arthur as well?" he asked in a polite way.

Doc chuckled.

I paused, then decided to watch where this pun would take us. "Feel free. Everybody else seems to."

"As Professor Gersema has explained it, he's managed to harness the waves of time, much as I do with water waves and river currents. This action moves the two of you through time in some sort of chronological method, like going down a river. Am I correct?"

Doc nodded, and then I quietly affirmed him with an "uh-huh," leaning into Russell Gersema with an even quieter, "No more is needed for him to know."

Doc nodded in agreement. Lou placed Dr. Greene's book on the table next to Putzi's book so that she could listen fully.

Then Captain Orrin Backus, motioning to volume 2 of Grant's memoirs, still held in my left hand, said almost innocently, "That looks like the same book that my brother has."

We looked around at one another and then back at him.

"Your brother?"

"By blood, yes, but not by character or integrity. I was actually surprised the last time we were together before the War of the Rebellion."

Doc moved us into the library and motioned for Backus to sit down comfortably in his stuffed chair. I pulled up a dining room chair and straddled it backward as I faced him. Doc stood ramrod straight and gave his total concentration to the riverboat captain.

"Go on."

"Lafayette—that is, my brother—and I had a mercantile business in Ohio before the war broke out. It was successful, and we operated well as partners, until the South seceded. I saw the coming war effort as a chance to serve my country. My brother, unfortunately, saw the rebellion as a chance to serve himself."

"How so?" Doc asked.

"He had no loyalty, except to making money."

"A war profiteer?" I asked.

"Yes, but worse than that. Lafayette made money selling weapons to the Rebels and cotton goods to the Yankees—food to one, medicine to the other. He didn't care where he went or with whom he dealt. We both had river backgrounds from our youth, along the Ohio River, the Maumee, the Mad River, the Black, the Chargin, and others. We knew how to navigate them, which had helped us bring items to our town before the war. Well, it helped my brother during the rebellion. He's become rich, very rich."

"So, tell us about the book he has … the one like this," I said as I held out Grant's volume 2 so that he could see it but not touch it.

"It's identical."

"When did you notice he first had it?" Doc asked.

"Before the rebellion."

"Really?"

"He traveled to New York City for us to consider doing retail business with some manufacturers there, which never amounted to anything. But on that trip, he did meet a publisher and a writer and came home with ideas on how we could make a lot of money. He seemed obsessed."

"And he had his copy of this book?" I held up the book again for him to ensure he was accurate.

"Yes." He peered intently at the title, then said, "Except it said 'volume 1' on it."

Lafayette Backus had indeed been to my townhouse. I reached into the back pocket of my pants, withdrew the folded copy paper photo, and unfolded it.

"Is this your brother?" I asked, knowing what the answer would be.

Orrin Backus looked in astonishment at the image, as well as at the paper on which it was printed.

Haltingly, he said, "Yes, uh, yes this is my brother." He paused, then turning the paper over in his hand, he asked, "What kind of … um … paper is this?"

"Dunder Mifflin twenty-pound copy paper" was on the tip of my tongue, and as I started to answer, a gasp from across the room interrupted what I thought was a really clever response—if only to myself.

"That's my signature, my penmanship," Lou said as she read the note to "Smith" from "Louise." She had just picked up the signed copy of *Hitler: The Missing Years*, turned a page, and exclaimed her astonishment.

Doc pointed at her. "You're *that* Louise?"

She looked at him as if to ask, "What are you talking about?"

Doc pointed to the book, spread wide open to the section where a woman's penmanship clearly marked a Christmas gift for a friend in 1948.

1913

The next few days saw the four of us—Russell Gersema, Lou Abraham, Orrin Backus, and me—put together a map of possible spacetime movements that followed Mr. Lafayette Backus from 1859 to 1913–14 to the present, including what was described by Putzi Hanfstaengl.

At first, I was concerned that providing the Captain (as we now called Orrin) with too much information would be wasting knowledge on a man of the nineteenth century, but Lou proved me wrong. Knowledge never hurt anyone. Figuring out how Lou returned to 1948, spent time with Putzi, and had him sign off on a book that was published nine years later was going to take some time to forecast *or* unravel, depending upon a person's point of view.

The Captain was a very smart man. He grasped the concepts quickly, in part due to his natural mathematical and navigational skills, which added to his incredibly quick mind and focused curiosity. He seemed to grasp the major themes of dimensional spacetime movement.

He read the books we had in our possession in our Vienna flat in January 1913, acquired from my first visit back to my townhouse. He found it fascinating that we had in our possession a book printed in 1885 with his signature in it, a book that he would one day own. He pored over volume 2 of Grant's book, seeing the penciled notations in his own handwriting.

Since, according to his own time frame, he was still in May 1864, much of what he'd experienced from 1861 to 1864 was completed and noted within the book in his own hand, published in 1885 and now read for the first time by him in 1913.

The things written in Grant's memoirs post-1864 were a mystery, his penciled notes even more so. The Captain's head was spinning, yet he kept pushing to learn more. He read with great relish the other books, especially Greene's *The Elegant Universe* and Dry's *The Newton Papers*.

But it was Putzi's book that connected the dots for him and for us as we mapped out the possibilities of his brother's movements—past and present. The Captain began helping Lou figure out how his brother may have intercepted her future life.

Not long after Lou and he had finished the first chapter of *Hitler: The Missing Years*, the Captain blurted out, "Arthur, I've got it! Putzi Hanfstaengl's family-run printing, publishing, and art store on Fifth Avenue in New York City is where my brother went in 1859. It was there that he met Putzi's family, which was half-American. I remember the family's odd last name."

Doc and I could see that his mind was racing forward and connecting dots.

The Captain continued, "I did some reading. Putzi's grandmother, born in Albany, New York, was General Sedgwick's cousin. She gave birth to Putzi's mother and tragically died just days later. The little girl was raised in Berlin, ultimately marrying Putzi's father, who had an international printing and publishing company with offices in Berlin, London, and New York City. Printers and publishers were drawn from all over."

"It's a fascinating biography, Captain, but how do Lafayette and Hitler's paths cross? And how does John Sedgwick's life intersect Putzi's fate?"

Doc, who had been pensively listening, said, "*Arthur*, is there a TC that runs through Fifth Avenue at any point?"

I just looked at him. *Arthur?* I thought.

He laughed.

Reluctantly, I did too as I shook my head and turned back to the pile of papers before me to check. I reviewed the rough drawings on the table and saw that there was a TC that ran right down the center of Fifth Avenue, cutting right through a short business block as the street veered to the left. I compared that spot with the address of the Hanfstaengl's family printing and publishing office and beamed.

"Ringo?" asked the Captain.

Doc, Lou, and I looked at one another. Then Doc and I realized what he was trying to say.

"Uh, yes, bingo!" I responded with a laugh. Apparently the story we shared with him about the Beatles left a slightly off impression with the Civil War riverboat captain. Nevertheless, I found it funny.

Doc picked up the momentum of the TC discovery. "Somehow, Lafayette stumbled across the TC near the publishing house and began his journey. But what could it have been?"

I asked, "What author's book or parchment could he have found that accidently allowed him to stumble into spacetime travel?"

Doc looked up from his many papers. "Two authors."

"Who?" I asked.

He looked at all three of us and said, "Mark Twain and Isaac Newton."

The Captain seemed familiar with the second author named and also somewhat familiar with the name of the first author. "My brother and I knew a river captain before the rebellion who called himself 'Mark Twain'—which means twelve feet deep—a kind of statement letting the crew know that it's still safe to navigate those waters. He was from Missouri, and we often crossed paths."

Lou didn't miss a beat. "Mark Twain? The original Mark Twain? Tom Sawyer's Mark Twain? We are going to meet him?"

I saw the light burn brightly in Dr. Russell Gersema's eyes.

Having discovered (and somewhat mastered) the what and where of spacetime dimensional travel, we were now about to enter into the world of Lafayette Backus and learn the how and why of this man's hunger to timelessly master wealth and overcome death, as if he were a god.

And science's greatest mind, Isaac Newton, would now prove that that particular job opening had long ago been filled.

Dr. Russell Gersema, physicist and dimensional spacetime traveler, was in his element ... almost.

He had his three ad hoc students—Captain Orrin Backus, Lou Abraham, and me—seated slightly in front of a large covered chalkboard in his library, all three students fully invested in learning. An element of the subject, however, seemed to bother him.

He began by giving us the largest picture imaginable before untangling the knotted web of events through which each (and then all) of us had so far traveled.

"Friends, we face a daunting challenge no other individuals have faced in history. It is no less an effort than attempting to hold back the sea roiling and tumbling within a pending tsunami, rushing and gaining speed, suddenly bursting onto an exposed continent, a place of land that should be a safe haven. In this case, the safe haven is the entire earth *and*," he said with a deep and penetrating look away from us, "the universe within which we on earth reside."

He picked up a tumbler of water and slowly drank the entire contents in one unbroken effort. It was as if his mind was connected to something other than what we could observe.

He finished, wiped his lips dry, and continued. "This is about science, not about religion. What I am about to share with you has been my greatest fear since I began studying these spacetime probabilities."

He paused with the look of a man strangely curious and otherworldly fearful, as one looking straight into the direction of his own possible demise.

"Let us begin," he said as he unveiled the sheet of fabric that hung over the large, remodeled chalkboard. There under that fabric and now in front of us was a series of large sheets of brown butcher paper, each attached to the other, all attached together to the chalkboard by wax. *Post-it Notes of unusual size*, I thought. Then I realized that the notes and all that we'd soon write on them could be brought back to the twenty-first century. Chalk dust simply gets erased.

A designated agenda with sub letters and numbers had been handwritten on large note sheets with the kind of coal artists use to sketch images. Doc started making additional notes on the paper as he talked.

"We came to Vienna, each with a somewhat unclear purpose for our attendance. Lou, yours was the clearest of purposes, though postgraduate students tend to always wonder, *What's next?* Don't they?"

Lou smiled and joined us in nodding.

Doc continued, "I'd love to say that I was bright enough to uncover this unique part of science. But I wasn't. I stumbled upon spacetime travel after years of reading Newton and Einstein, learning about DNA and TCs, and reading Dr. Brian Greene's work, though none of them intimated such travel was possible. I knew it was both possible and probable. Now I'm also reading Max Abraham as well," he said with a smile to Lou. She smiled back.

They seem to be smiling at each other a lot, I noted.

"It was my focus as a physicist to discover more about spacetime travel. I wanted to learn what I could do to save my family from Hitler and the Nazis. My passion as a Jew pushed me deeper into action."

Lou, nodding to encourage him, said, "That makes sense. Our Jewish families were wiped out."

Doc acknowledged Lou's comment about their heritage. He then continued. "Author, you came unknowingly into January

1913. Thinking that you accidently met me at Café Central, you walked out of your then-present-day life and into the now-present early lives of Hitler, Stalin, Trotsky, Tito, Lenin, and Freud. There was nothing accidental about us meeting."

He paused, as if coming clean with something. "I needed two things from you."

The air hung heavy as he paused.

I cut through the heaviness with a smile. "Yes, you did. You needed a brilliant though truly humble author, and you needed a plucky comic relief."

For the first time in this setting, I saw the twinkle in Dr. Gersema's eyes return. It had slowly faded away during recent events.

"Well, okay, those and two other things. I needed a religious man who could help me understand Newton's almost incessantly irrational belief in a creator. Your books were vulnerable and raw. Prior to reading your works, I'd never seen that in the lives of any men of faith about whom I was aware." He paused as if embarrassed.

I suppose I blushed as well.

He continued, "It became obvious to the casual observer that we needed another physicist—even a young one—and, Lou, you walked into our lives. But more than that, somehow you were destined to be with us. How else can any of us explain that you, Lou, are the Louise of Christmas 1948? And that the *you* of the future will meet Putzi, have dinner with him, and place a handwritten note to some mysterious *Smith* inside a book that will not even be published for an additional seven years in 1957—yet a book I'd need in 1913? In ordinary time and space, this would make no sense. But with TCs and spacetime travel, it is as it is. We just don't know the reason for your future involvement."

Lou shook her head and said, "I'll be in my late fifties on that particular Christmas in 1948." She paused, then added, "I wonder what I'll look like."

Sensing a need to move on, the Captain asked, "What else did you want?"

Using the piece of coal he had been writing with, Doc pointed at the two of us. "I want the one particular copy of U. S. Grant's memoirs to help me travel through the dimensions and construct the Grant-Sedgwick-Putzi-Hitler equation. I need the DNA and/or the autograph of Ulysses S. Grant, Captain. I had come to the conclusion that someone else was also traveling through spacetime to thwart my efforts." He looked at Orrin Backus and added, "The fact that you were the original owner of Grant's work and had signed volume 1 was vital to me. I needed a backup plan. Captain, you were that plan."

He continued, "Once the first volume was taken from the Author's townhouse, I was at a loss—until I realized your DNA was still very much in volume 2, due to your habit of penciling notations throughout both volumes. I discovered it purely by accident."

"An accident of history?" the Captain asked.

"A mad accident of history," Doc stated, looking at him. "I could not put my finger on who was thwarting us until you saw clearly who the antagonist was."

"My brother." He looked down at the floor.

"Yes."

Turning to the first sheet of butcher paper, our resident physicist began connecting the dots.

"Isaac Newton was, by all accounts, one of the most brilliant men who ever lived. His contribution to science is so multifaceted that most scientists since his day would be hard-pressed to debate his influence. Yet ..." He paused and picked up one of the books we'd brought back from my townhouse.

He turned pages until he arrived at page 73. "Allow me to read from Sarah Dry's incredible investigative work, *The Newton Papers,* published in 2014 by Oxford Press. This is an incident in 1855 involving Newton biographer David Brewster, from his book, *Memoirs of the Life of Isaac Newton.*"

The Captain, Lou, and I settled into our comfortable, plush chairs to listen.

He began reading:

> The matter of Newton's religion vexed Brewster, but he thought it pointless to hide from the public 'that which they have long suspected, and must sooner or later known' though he admitted to having 'touched lightly and unwillingly, on a subject so tender.' Rather than trying to dispute or justify Newton's beliefs, Brewster decided to publish the relevant manuscripts and let his readers make their own judgment, urging them, however, to recall that 'by the great Teacher alone can truth be taught.' Only God himself, 'at his tribunal' argued Brewster could explain how so much anti-Trinitarianism chaff could have mixed with the golden wheat that was Newton's science.
>
> For Brewster, the question of Newton's faith was paramount. And he was not alone. Even in the middle of the nineteenth century, several troubling issues continued to surround the question of Newton's religion. Had Newton held a lifelong interest in theological matters or had it been merely the product of his dotage, the feeble imaginings of a weakened mind?

Dr. Russ Gersema paused, closing Sarah Dry's book just slightly.

"This *vexes* me to no end as well," he stated. "I find it so totally irreconcilable that the most brilliant man who ever lived saw the Christian faith as key to his own life. Newton's published works are incredible. His scholarly mathematical work, *The Principia*, still stands as a foundation for modern math and science. He wrote much more. Scientific minds, including Einstein, Max Planck, Max Abraham, and others, saw Newton as—pardon the expression—*an apostle of truth* and all that is good in science. It all fits nicely together with how science operates, orderly and functionally." He paused, looking as though he didn't want to continue.

"And?" I said, prompting him.

"And scientists across the ages thought we had read all that Newton had written. However, as Dry presents in her work, there were additional papers of Newton's that languished for centuries, with only a handful of academics having investigated them. Although selected parts were published, the full body of his additional work was not. A handful of attempts, including work done by David Brewster, moved the private papers closer to being published. But time marched on, and interest in these papers waned."

I prompted him once again. "Until when?"

"Well, believe it or not, until twenty-three years *from now*—in 1936—when the full component of Isaac Newton's private papers will be auctioned off in London and much of his private thoughts will be exposed to the world at large and the scientific community in particular. Those papers show a man who tried incessantly to authenticate alchemy—the act of turning one metal into another—*and* who believed in a creator. Both theories were unsettling to scientific minds."

"Even Einstein was shocked by what Newton wrote," Doc stated as he looked for a piece of paper he had set aside on his table. "Here it is."

Lou moved forward, as if to listen more intently.

"Listen to what Albert Einstein said in a letter to Abraham Yahuda, one of the men who in 1936 bid and won ownership of Newton's writings on religion: 'Newton's writings on biblical subjects seem to me especially interesting because they provide deep insight into the characteristic intellectual features and working methods of this important man. The divine origin of the Bible is for Newton absolutely certain, a conviction that stands in curious contrast to the critical skepticism that characterizes his attitude toward the churches. From this confidence stems the firm conviction that the seemingly obscure parts of the Bible must contain important revelations, to illuminate which one need only decipher its symbolic language.'"

"A kind of code?" I asked.

"Yes, a Bible code—a Jewish-Christian code. And that was said about the smartest man who ever lived by probably the second smartest man who lived," Doc said.

Shaking his head side to side, Doc continued, "Isaac Newton's scientific method for discovering the deepest, most profound areas of science was used to study the Bible. He poured himself into a book of myths, old sayings, and ancient history as if it was as real as the discovery of gravity."

I squinted my eyes once again, this time unsettled by Doc's unintentional attempt at shaming a book revered by millions. My inner Liam Neeson was flinching.

The Captain broke in, saying, "Why would Newton be called brilliant by people in one area and dismissed as a fool by those same people in another area? Wasn't *The Principia* as well as these other papers about God written at the same time?"

"Yes, they were." The scientist in Dr. Gersema seemed in conflict with his own curious mind. The battle exposed itself to all of us but most importantly to himself.

Silence then enveloped us. Lou squirmed as well.

Doc seemed to break free of the Captain's logical question, his own answer, and the equally clear implications. "Captain, many of us in the scientific community cannot accept theology as a part of a world constructed by mathematics and physics."

"Why not?" the Captain asked.

"It's because of evolution. The world in the near future will more fully accept it, along with the other branches of science ... and with great passion and in great numbers, rather than accepting orthodox Christian faith. Its founder—"

Captain Orrin Backus interrupted. "Its founder is Charles Darwin. He published *The Origin of Man* just a few years ago in 1859. Well, just a few years ago for me," he said with a smile.

Doc and I were shocked that the riverboat captain knew of Darwin.

"That book changed the direction of my brother, Lafayette, from the moment he got his hands on it during his trip to New York City in 1859. It made him lose his religion; our parents raised us as Methodists in Ohio. And from Darwin's book, my brother began to think only about the survival of the fittest—only of this world and not of the next."

A quiet hush divided us.

Lou said, "Evolution doesn't diminish the value of people of faith and what they hold true, does it?"

The Captain concurred but held up a finger, as if to ask a further question.

Lou continued, nonetheless, "I am a daughter of Abraham, literally. And as a Jew, I was raised in Torah, understood the scriptures, and had my bat mitzvah at the appropriate age. My uncle Max was a practicing Jew, as was our whole family."

The Captain spoke up again. "Agreed, yet we have to look at the very first book of Torah—the book of Genesis—and in it, mankind's mother and father were created in a moment, in a stroke of time. There was an event and therefore no process, no evolving."

Lou gently responded, "Yes, Captain, you are right that in Hebrew the Torah says our two original parents were named Adama and Chava. His name means earth, and it's from the dust of the ground from which he was formed. From Adama came his wife. Her name is associated with the Hebrew word *chaya*, or living. So, from her came all living things."

The Captain concurred with Lou and said something extraordinary—something that I had never heard as an evangelical in the twenty-first century but that must have been an accepted idea in the nineteenth century.

"The change of animals all happened before man was ever created. It's called the old earth belief, and many held to it in the 1850s. Dr. Darwin's problem was that in order to have his evolution theory work, he could not connect it to theology and therefore would not allow a discussion of an old earth to occur. In his theory, there was only this period or dimension of time and no other."

The Captain continued, "Professor, you've brought me through time and space to join you as we search for my brother. In my world of 1864, I've seen tens of thousands of men slaughtered in battles across those several fields in those United States. Not a single young man cried out for science as they faced eternity. They cried out for their parents and finally for God."

"Yes, Captain, that was then. This is now," he said hesitantly. It appeared to me that he didn't fully believe what he was saying.

He continued, "Those of us in science look for facts, not faith, to give us truth. That's what Darwin did."

Lou, thoughtful as ever, added as if to herself, "Yet without even considering an old earth idea."

The Captain continued, "I suppose, even in my limited time with you both as physicists, I can understand why facts mean so much to you. In my world of river navigation, facts are—how did Mr. Brewster describe it in his writings—*paramount*. I understand that. I'm really not a religious man; it was just what I grew up with and what I learned. Obviously you now know that my brother is not religious. Yet there seems to be more to life on earth than what we knew in 1859 or 1864 or even in 1913, right?"

Doc responded, "Well, science is a continuing discipline of new discoveries and new bases for truth. We've learned a lot since then."

"Did the scientists of the future realize that many of their old beliefs were unfounded?" the Captain asked with an air of honest innocence in his voice. Lou leaned in closer to hear Doc's response.

"We did," Doc responded. "In those same private papers of Newton, we uncovered his wrong belief that certain branches of science were interwoven. For example, the forerunner to chemistry, alchemy, was a medieval chemical science aimed at transmuting base metals into gold. He believed in it and worked hard but unsuccessfully in this."

I said, "In addition, alchemy also looked for a universal cure for disease and a means to prolong life. That seems worthwhile."

Doc concurred and added, "An interesting theory, yet he looked foolish."

"Since that was found to be false, all of Mr. Newton's works became false too?" the Captain asked.

"Uh, no."

"I'm confused," the Captain said. "Who makes the decision to accept his brilliance on one issue and then refer to his thinking as foolish at another level?"

"Science does. We investigate, we experiment, we repeat or duplicate the experiments, and then we deduce the results. From that scientific method, we find truthful results. Almost all other results are dismissed."

"On the river, we call that eliminating a side eddy. The river continues to go downstream. And a good captain will steer toward what works. Did Newton do that?"

"Yes, that's a good expression," the clever twenty-first-century physicist said to the nineteenth-century self-taught riverboat captain.

"So Mr. Newton's work on religion could still be somewhat accurate and valuable, even if the alchemy experiments failed?"

"Um, I suppose so."

Lou and I just sat and watched.

The Captain said, "I don't know about the world in the twenty-first century, but in the America of the 1850s, we've just had widespread religious revival in the wilderness. They've called these get-togethers 'camp meetings.' Because of them, many people now believe that the War of the Rebellion will be what the Bible talks about for the end of the world."

Doc's eyes must have flattened in response, as if to say, "Every generation foolishly thinks that sort of thing."

There was a very long pause.

The Captain had seen the visual flat line response from Doc. "Obviously, it didn't end."

All four of us unexpectantly laughed. Lou seemed particularly thankful that humor had interrupted the intense discussion.

The Captain continued, "I have two final questions. Did Isaac Newton write about end-times from his study of the Bible? You know, when the world *would* end."

I could see discomfort return to Doc. Lou picked up on Doc's unsettledness.

"Yes, he did," Doc answered.

Then both men looked at each other, the one who survived navigating rivers in nineteenth-century American wartime as well as the one who navigated spacetime through the future, unsure if anything would survive. The Captain broke the silence. "What's the earliest year that Newton said the world could end?"

Doc looked down at the floor, then up at the ceiling. Lou pressed him. "Dr. Gersema, what year?"

He looked straight at her and in a monotone voice replied, "Two thousand sixty."

12

1913

It was finally on the table.

This was the reason for the deep-seated sadness and discomfort that Captain Orrin Backus, Lou Abraham, and I had seen in Dr. Russell Gersema. He literally felt the weight of the world upon his shoulders, if Isaac Newton was correct.

The Captain and I could sense Doc's level of internal pressure; he could not think his way out of this situation. He needed to determine whether Newton's prognosis for the end of the world fell into the internationally respected mathematical side of this brilliant man's mind or whether it was another offshoot of his discredited side, judged that way by his scientific peers over the ages.

Doc looked defeated and hopeless, not wanting to believe in an end-of-the-world scenario but facing it nonetheless because it was the brainchild of Isaac Newton.

I stood up and took the coal from Doc's hand, motioning for him to take the chair I had just been in. I had something to say.

"Friends, let's keep focused on the things we know at this point and draw conclusions from those facts." I turned to the board with butcher paper attached by quarter-sized blobs of candle wax and began to write.

I scribbled the following points on the next available large sheet of paper:

1. No belief in the Bible.

I said, "Since Lafayette does not believe in a divine creator, how can he believe in an equally biblical apocalypse—an end to that creation? He doesn't. If life continues without a divine purpose, why worry about the end of times? Therefore, he doesn't care about Newton's 2060 prediction." Then I wrote the second point.

2. He believes he can live forever.

I continued, "As long as he maintains control of spacetime travel, he believes he'll keep living, right? He'll always live in the *now* of time. Eliminating trespassers stops all threats to his life, allowing him to have neither past nor future. He just *is*." I turned a final time to the board and wrote:

3. We may be trespassers and threats to him.

"It could be that Lafayette sees us—and any others who will follow—as trespassers and ultimately as threats to his life. We're not trying to find *him*; he may be trying to find us."

"Why has he not simply walked up and killed us, as you did Hitler?" Lou asked.

Doc responded, "He may have already done so, and the world turned out poorly for him, so he's letting us live. He may still need something we currently have; he may indeed be waiting and watching us."

The Captain said, "My brother may be following us?"

Doc nodded as I responded, "That's my theory, Captain. I believe it to be sound and that we'll find traces of him having been around us. We need to determine what it is that he wants from one or all of us as we move forward."

I tore off this sheet of paper and stuck it to the closest wall in the library. As I looked up, I noticed the writings that had been hanging higher on the wall since the first time I walked into the library. Same butcher paper, same coal letters, obviously a part of Doc's processing method.

"Okay, are we all agreed on these three points?" I asked.

The Captain looked pensively at the scribbled points and then responded, "Even with your theory about my brother following us, I believe you have distilled our dilemma down to its three basic suppositions. And I believe your points are accurate, though there may still be things coming at us about which we cannot yet anticipate. I know my brother."

"Yes, yes, of course," I answered and then looked over at Doc.

He sat patiently, deeply thinking. I noticed that he no longer showed any of the agitation or frustration that had clouded his thinking prior to my summary.

As was his custom, he crossed his legs and in an intentionally cavalier fashion began to flick lint off his pressed gabardine slacks. Then he leaned forward, looking upward above where I had adhered my three-point overview to the library wall.

He pointed to a particular piece of butcher paper hanging near the top of the wall, amid quite a few other papers and maps stuck to the wall. In a slow, steady voice, he said, "The answer's there, my friends."

We looked at him and then at one another. Doc effortlessly stood and almost glided toward the moveable ladder; holding it and sliding it to the edge of the bookcase, he ascended it.

At the top of the library atop the ladder, he stopped and read from a single sheet of large paper as he peeled the sheet from the wall. "Mark Twain: Hawaii, U. S. Grant, and Austria."

We had no context for whatever it was Doc was saying.

"Mark Twain?" the Captain asked.

Doc responded as he descended the ladder; sheet in hand, "You and *Arthur* have him to thank for the book you both own."

"Grant's memoirs?" we responded in unison.

"Yes," he answered, having hopped from the last rung, feet now firmly on the floor in front of the ladder.

"Take a look at the book we have and read the publisher's name."

The Captain picked up volume 2 and read from the spine of the book, "Charles L. Webster & Company."

"That's correct," Doc responded as he regained his seat, placing the now neatly folded butcher-block paper on his lap, covering up those gabardine slacks.

"The '& Company' is Mark Twain," Doc stated.

The Captain looked nonplused. I was intrigued. "Hmmm."

Then, as if for effect, Dr. Gersema looked at us.

"He lives here in Vienna, just up the street and seventeen years ago."

He smiled as he looked at the lovely Jewish postgraduate student and the two believers in Jesus standing before him. He took out a cigar and lit it. "Twain wrote some interesting things when he lived here. Some biographers say it may have been his most productive time of writing. One piece in particular stands out for me."

"Really?" Lou asked. "Which one?"

"A little ditty titled *Conversations with Satan.*"

13

1897

There are three cards in modern times that people play when conflict comes their way and they want to win.

Two cards are interchangeable, though one is used more often than the other. The third card stands on its own. No matter what the discussion, no matter the debate, once any of the three cards is played, the game folds. It's not always clear who *wins* the game, but it is abundantly clear who *ends* the game.

Use the words *Nazi* and *Hitler*, and all forward progress ends.

As pure evil as both words are by themselves, they seem to sometimes fall into the unique category that ancient Romans so ably captured in their language. Humor trumps seriousness by reducing it to the absurd: reductio ad absurdum.

Leave it to Jerry Seinfeld's television show to best trivialize the first word by including it in a comedy skit: "The Soup Nazi."

Funny, dismissive, absurd.

The pain of millions of lives lost in WWII is reduced to a skit about a mean-spirited delicatessen owner in New York City who refuses to serve customers.

When in Rome and NYC, reductio ad absurdum.

Hitler's name appears to be less pliable in the halls of humor.

Yet, when Mel Brooks made his directorial debut in 1967 with his screenplay *The Producers*, the absurd reduction of the Third Reich's Führer to a character in a comedy film was highlighted by the uplifting and sarcastic song, "Springtime for Hitler and Germany." An Academy Award followed.

I mentioned three cards.

So, what other name can claim an even more evil title than the two we've just covered? Mark Twain seemed to know which name would best represent his thoughts, and he chose it specifically in his piece: Satan.

He did so in Vienna in 1897.

Throughout his career, Sam Clemens toyed with writing his autobiography. Even as a thirty-one-year-old journalist in 1866 Hawaii, living in a shack just off the main trail at the southern tip near the dusty road that circumnavigated the big island, he believed an autobiography would one day come. It was hit and miss, though, over the years. This apparent inconsistent goal left future biographers combing through piles and piles of papers and mounds of manuscripts to eventually publish volume 1 of Mark Twain's autobiography, one hundred years after his death. He sanctioned that release in his will.

While in Vienna in the late 1890s, the consummate humorist wrote, "A man cannot tell the whole truth about himself, even if convinced that what he wrote would never be seen by others … for that reason I confine myself to drawing the portraits of others."

Battling sadness and the death of his daughter, financial collapse, and what appeared to be the end of his writing career, both Samuel Clemens and his deeply depressed twin, Mark Twain, were at the edge of despair. He was unable to write and was in that state for a long time.

Then, one evening in Vienna, he began drawing a portrait of a mysterious stranger that visited his main character, Theodor, and had a detailed conversation with him about humankind.

Through much discussion and a clear display of power, the object of Twain's portrait says the following to young Theodor:

> "Life itself is only a vision, as dream. I am but a dream—your dream, creature of your imagination. In a moment you will have realized this, then you will banish me from your visions and I shall dissolve into the nothingness out of which you made me.
>
> "It is true, that which I have revealed to you; there is no God, no universe, no human race, no earthly life, no heaven, no hell. It is all a dream—a grotesque and foolish dream. Nothing exists but you. And you are but a thought—a vagrant thought, a useless thought, a homeless thought, wandering forlorn among the empty eternities!"

Twain's world was both stopping and restarting in Vienna in 1897. His thoughts were scribbled down in his flat in Vienna a short distance from Café Central, a decade and a half before I would eventually meet Dr. Gersema, Captain Backus, and Adolf Hitler and see the world turn on a different axis in spacetime.

It was from this time forward that Mark Twain's world began to change.

I have always wondered why Mark Twain regained his sense of purpose and began to write again. Why in Vienna?

With specificity and purpose as he withdrew bundled sheets of paper with an autograph on its top page from a file that had previously held the Einstein paper, Doc announced, "Friends, let's meet Mark Twain right before he meets Franz Joseph, the emperor of Austria and the king of Hungary."

Mark Twain lived in Vienna and its surrounding area from September 1897 to May 1899, a period longer in his life than spent in any country except America.

In Europe, Twain's family appeared to live as wealthy nomads—overall, for almost four years, enjoying the odd eccentricities of the different European countries. The actual reason for their European residency was the comparatively low cost of living. Their family finances were strained almost to a breaking point.

Mark Twain's American business creditors were pursuing him.

Business failures had plagued him to the degree that he lost most of what he had made as a fabulously successful international writer, along with a large portion of his wife's inheritance.

His publishing company was a failure as were the printing inventions into which he had invested millions of dollars. He wrote well; he just did not invest well—unless it was in travel.

In 1891, he and his family escaped to England, Germany, France, and Italy. They forged this unsettled adventure together for four years before returning home to America.

But not for long, as he invested again in travel.

This time, Twain and his family embarked on a world tour midway through the decade. Ultimately, he regained his financial stability and paid off many of his creditors. Their world tour was a great success.

It was at that moment of success that Twain and his family returned to Europe near the very end of the 1890s and settled in Vienna. They resided for nine months in Vienna's Hotel Metropol, taking in the beauty of the city and enjoying dinner houses, opera houses, and coffee houses. Café Central's beauty and location held him in its sway.

For four more months, Twain and his family lived in Kaltenleutgeben, in the lovely Villa Paulhof near the woods of Vienna, seeking "water cure treatments" for his wife, Livy, who had long been in ill health. People came from multiple countries to receive electrical energy and water treatments; the small spa did big business. The area emits 16,000 Bovis biophoton energy units, with telluric currents passing nearby.

Telluric current number one ushered us from our flat in Vienna in January 1913 to the front yard of a small first-floor apartment with a lovely flower garden in full bloom. We could hear some hammering inside the apartment. Doc was confident as the four of us of us approached the door. He held tightly a bundle of papers in his left fist as he knocked on the door with his right. It was the quintessential rhythm of one American calling out to another American, the first five notes of music that have both a call *and* an expected response to them.

Surprising the Captain, Lou, and me, Doc sang as he knocked, "Shave and a haircut …"

The construction work inside stopped, yet I could not detect any movement toward the front door.

So Doc did it again—only louder, knocking and singing, "Shave and a haircut …"

Firm footfalls hurried to the door. A loud, resonating, southern Missouri–accented voice drew near to the front door as it swung open.

He sang, "Two bits," adding the corresponding amount of knocks on the doorjamb.

"Now, *that's* the door knock of an American!" the figure said.

Before us stood the relatively healthy sixty-two-year-old version of America's most famous humorist with a smile on his face, his wild white hair everywhere, and a cigar clenched in his teeth. He was sweaty and wearing work clothes and gloves, the type worn when tackling remodeling projects or gardening at home on a Saturday.

"Americans in Austria!" he shouted with a smile as he removed the cigar. He paused and then said, "You're not creditors, are you?"

Doc answered with a clear voice and an extended, outstretched hand, "No, we are not. We're fans of yours from way back …"

With a work glove on, Twain shook Doc's hand and in a grand gesture, with a sweep of his other gloved hand, said, "Fellow

Americans, enter and welcome to Villa Paulhof—our home away from home." Removing his work gloves and taking a rag out of his back pocket, he wiped off the dust and grit and extended his right hand. "I'm Sam Clemens. Who do I have the honor of meeting?"

Doc started to answer but was interrupted.

"Sam Clemens?" Orrin Backus called out. "Samuel Clemens from Missouri? The riverboat pilot?"

Doc and I looked at each other, more surprised than embarrassed, though blushing nonetheless. This wasn't quite the plan.

Twain responded, "Yes, that was a long time ago. Do we know each other from the river?"

"Sure as tarnation do!" the Captain said and then turned toward us suddenly. "I thought we were meeting someone named Mark Twain. Not Captain Clemens!" he said, his voice raised in surprise and joy.

Twain bent at the waist toward Captain Orrin Backus, examining the guest's somewhat youthful facial features, obviously a much younger man than the humorist and former riverboat pilot was now.

Slowly Twain's eyes widened. "Now ain't that the beatingest language you ever did hear!"

Doc and I flinched, not knowing what he meant.

Captain Backus responded, "It's 100 percent certified to a Philadelfy lawyer."

Twain said, "I'll hang up my fiddle, and you can sass me!"

What? I looked at Doc again; both of us were lost. We couldn't understand what these two men clearly *did* understand.

The Captain said, "Well, Sam, it's sure a huckleberry above anyone's persimmon to see you again!" Both men shook hands while embracing like two long-lost fraternity brothers.

Twain said, "Dad gum it all, how can you be in your forties and me in my sixties, and we knew each other when we were young together?" He looked at us and leaned on the open door, wiping the remaining dirt off his fingers. "Well, it appears we have a mystery on our hands. Care to come in and have some southern-style lemonade and solve it together?" The world's most well-known author and humorist walked arm in arm into his Austrian home with his fellow riverboat captain. Doc and I followed behind, unnamed and unknown.

As we entered his cottage apartment, he said, "The Germans and Austrians do know how to brew beer but are lost when it comes to making American lemonade." He laughed the laugh of a man happy to meet new friends from his old hometown. "Try and find lemons in Austria! But my Livy does."

Twain set aside his work gloves and rag and invited us to sit at the kitchen table. He moved over to the sink and washed his hands under the old-fashioned indoor water spigot, pumping the lever handle as he talked. "By golly, it's good to have you here." After wiping off the water from his hands, he reached over to a pitcher of lemonade and some glasses. "Livy made this for me in the late morning, in case I got thirsty after doing some carpentry work. Food and drink always taste better when we share it." He smiled at us and poured a little bit of America for us to enjoy. We drank it.

Our captain smiled and wiped some residue from his upper lip and said to the *other* captain, "I knew a Mark Twain during our time on the river, but that wasn't you."

Taking his seat, Twain took a sip of lemonade, paused, and then looked at Doc, Lou, and me, apparently determining whether it was safe for him to open up on the subject.

It was.

He turned to his newest *old* friend. "Captain Backus, you are correct. Since I became famous, I've told people that another Mississippi riverboat captain once owned this particular name and I merely, to quote myself, 'laid violent hands upon it.'"

The next thing I heard surprised me. Doc interrupted the pleasant banter and stated, "But that wasn't accurate, was it, Mr. Clemens?"

Twain spun in his chair toward Doc. "What? How dare you." He paused to change the direction of the conversation. "Who are you other folks?"

Ignoring the question, Doc pressed his advantage. "It wasn't accurate. That never happened, did it?"

The air grew thick.

For once, Mark Twain, noted speaker and international communicator, remained quiet.

I looked at Doc with an expression of terror, wondering why he was so abruptly changing the tone and temperature of this formerly pleasant meeting. He shot me a glance of total calm and assurance. Lou fastened her eyes on Sam, as if to tell herself she was really even there—in front of Mark Twain.

"Mr. Clemens, my name is Dr. Russell Gersema. I am a physicist, and I am from the future, as is my friend," he said, pointing at me.

The Captain said, "His name is Arthur."

I looked down at the floor.

Doc continued, "And this is Lou Abraham, a postgraduate student in physics at the University of Vienna. I know you are a man of science and you're also fascinated by spiritualism. We have a tale to tell you—one that even you as an author could not dream up—and I need to ensure that you clearly understand my veracity and accuracy at this very moment. And we need your help."

Twain sat stunned, moving toward confused.

Doc continued, "Please suspend your disbelief and allow me to offer two examples that will prove my truthfulness and that of my three friends." Without truly seeking Mark Twain's approval, Doc continued.

"First, your pen name." He opened up the collection of papers he brought and withdrew from it a printed copy of an article from 2018 by Daniel Hernandez, written for a periodical called the *Mark Twain Journal*. "Kevin Mac Donnell, a rare-book dealer in Austin, Texas, discovered an 1861 magazine sketch that offers the first fact-based theory on your name. Mr. Hernandez writes, 'It suggests Clemens found his pseudonym in a popular humor journal, then invented the riverboat story to promote his Missouri roots.'"

Doc paused, then stated, "The journal was *Vanity Fair*, and you read it quite often, didn't you?"

Now it was Mark Twain's time to look at the floor.

Doc said, "They're right, aren't they?"

Twain looked up and nodded his head yes. "I liked the name. It reminded me of my time on the river. I made up the story about borrowing it from another pilot to add color to the tale. I suppose it was an author's prerogative, and it was a lie that I kept telling." His shoulders slumped, but he looked up at us. "How in the world did you find that out?"

I couldn't resist. "I Googled it."

Twain, Lou, and the Captain looked at me, all with questioning, furrowed eyebrows. Now it was my time to speak understandable gibberish to the two riverboat captains—*ha*. I suppose I wanted to see their reactions.

Doc looked directly into Twain's eyes. "Mr. Clemens, I didn't bring this up to call you a liar; I said it to grab your attention so I could prove that we're from the future in a different type of spacetime."

Twain rocked back in his chair, forcing it even farther onto its two hind legs and just bored his eyes into the three of us.

After a minute or so, he heartily laughed, as if having discovered something he should have already known. "You think you're Hank Morgan, don't you?"

We all stopped. He seemed to suddenly have *us* on the defensive.

My mind as an author went into hyperdrive. *Morgan, Hank Morgan, Mark Twain, characters, time travel.* I suddenly understood: Hank Morgan was the protagonist in Twain's book, *A Connecticut Yankee in King Arthur's Court.* I thought, *Oh my gosh. He thinks we're fans of his who have taken to heart—a little too closely—his own time travel book and believe it to be true.*

I now knew where to go with this.

I leaned into Mark Twain's space and motioned with my index finger for him to come closer to me. His chair roared back onto four legs, and he leaned toward me. I came close to his left ear and whispered something.

He turned his head and looked into my face and nodded.

I turned to Doc. "Okay, Dr. Gersema, show him your other piece of evidence."

Doc opened the bundle of papers until he found a small slip of yellowed paper.

"You haven't yet finished your carpentry work, have you?"

Twain looked at Doc. "No, I have not."

Pointing to a small gaping hole in the wall at shoulder level next to the fireplace in the living room, Doc asked, "Were you about to place some papers and a note into that opening and seal it up?"

Twain responded, "Why, yes I was."

"Do you have them nearby? If so, may I see them?"

Twain reached across the table to a small pile of papers, disheveled and unstacked. He moved it toward Doc, like a gambler advancing his total winnings to the center of a table, saying in a sense, "I'm all in."

Dr. Russell Gersema received them, quickly finding what he was looking for.

Picking up a scrap of paper, he read it out loud to all of us. "'It's best to tell the truth when nothing else occurs to you. Mark Twain.'"

Twain smiled broadly as if having been caught in the act and said, "I thought I'd leave a little memento for some Austrian to find in the future."

Captain Backus and Lou laughed with him, though Twain's side glance toward me belied a slight hesitancy. I winked at him, as if to call the hand.

Doc smiled too. "Well, you were successful. His name is Jorg Wollman. He and his American wife, Anne, will live here in 2008 and uncover your treasury of papers while remodeling. They were kind enough to sell one of them to me."

Then, Doc did what only Doc can do.

He took the newly scribbled note from Clemens's pile on the table and placed it in his left hand, as he opened up his right, unveiling that exact piece of paper, only yellowed now after a century of being behind the wall.

Doc looked into Mark Twain's eyes again and, without glancing at the message on the paper, said, "It's best to tell the truth when nothing else occurs to you."

14

1897

The afternoon quickly became evening as "border state southerner" Mark Twain, the creator of his Connecticut time and space traveler Hank Morgan, sat listening to his Austrian court of four Yankees unveil this tale. Pages of paper flowed as he piloted his pencil. This former riverboat captain turned author was undeterred and followed every bend in the river and plot twist. He understood the significance of what was now before him.

We all soon became familiar with one another on a first-name basis. Mr. Samuel Clemens, known to the world as Mark Twain, became only "Sam" as we talked on and on.

He stopped at one point and, taking a drag on his half-smoked cigar, asked us the question we knew was coming, "What becomes of my wife, my family, and me?"

"May I start first with the future finances of your family?" Doc answered.

Sam exhaled a large cloud of smoke and nodded an emphatic *yes*.

"It's going to be painful to listen to, Sam." Doc moved forward without asking or receiving further approval from Sam; he unpacked the incredibly poor record of financial mismanagement that Sam Clemens had done up to the year 1897, as if to prove that what followed would have an equal amount of credibility.

It did.

The pain to us as witnesses of this man's history, of hearing the name of his now-defunct publishing company, Charles L. Webster & Co. was intense, as was hearing how terribly wrong many other financial decisions he had made were, forcing Sam's head to fall lower and lower onto his chest.

"And people wonder why I'm a bitter, angry man in so much of what I write. Sarcastic and cutting, my Livy calls it. My God, no wonder. Look at what a mess I've made of my life and the life of my family."

I did not interrupt but waited till Sam was finished. "Yes, that's true. But what if you could travel through spacetime and correct the things you failed in." I paused for effect, knowing exactly where I was headed. "To have a rain check for your life?"

Sam turned his head upward at the sound of the baseball term.

As an author and a baseball fan, I knew much of Sam Clemens's enjoyment of baseball. He was an early supporter of the first major league, the National Association, founded after the Civil War. In the mid-1870s, he was a regular attendee as the Hartford Dark Blues played the Chicago White Stockings, the Middletown Mansfields, Philadelphia Athletics, New York Mutuals, and eighteen other teams, ending always with their rivals, the Boston Red Stockings.

"Think of it this way, and please pardon my quoting of you in front of you."

Sam's head was now fully raised. I could see wonderment in his face as he tried to overlay his love of baseball onto the pathos of his financial life. He signaled his approval for me to cite a quote.

I paused and then from memory recited, "'Two hundred and five dollars reward. At the great baseball match on Tuesday, while I was engaged in hurrahing, a small boy walked off with an English-made brown silk umbrella belonging to me, and forgot to bring it back. I will pay $5 for the return of that umbrella in good condition to my home on Farmington Avenue. I do not want the boy (in an active state) but will pay two hundred dollars for his remains. Samuel L. Clemens.'"

We all laughed, including Sam.

"Did I write that?" he asked, smirking.

"Indeed you did. I memorized it in the 1960s when I was a little league player and had lots of time on the bench due to my lack of skill on the field. I suppose I learned the value of wordsmithing as I sat the bench. You probably kept me from stealing another man's English-made, brown silk umbrella."

Samuel Clemens sat up, adjusted himself as if putting on his Mark Twain persona, and said to me, a late-in-life author of unimpressive accomplishments, "Well, Arthur, I must read one of your books."

"I'll make sure you have one." It was the best I could choke out in my veiled emotion.

Sam took the moment to refill everyone's lemonade glasses.

Doc picked up the lead as we moved in a way that mirrored his earlier fondness for fairness and the Beatles. "Sam, when you lived in Hawaii just after the war in 1866, did you buy any land for an investment?"

"Heavens no! Who's going to prosper purchasing land on those godforsaken but thoroughly lovely Sandwich Islands? It takes too long to get there by ship. The temperature *is* warm, yet the land so overgrown and unruly. No, no. There's no way I planted money into that soil, although I will say I planted a tree that blossomed there. It was a monkeypod; I planted it from seeds in a little place called Waiohinu."

Doc continued, "And did you invest in the Boston Red Stockings baseball team?"

"Nope, I wouldn't put money into that godforsaken, worthless opponent to my beloved Hartford Dark Blues." Sam took another puff from his cigar.

Like a cross-examining prosecuting attorney, Doc probed a bit deeper. "And furthermore, when you hired Charles L. Webster when he was thirty years old as your business manager and then your full partner in the publishing business, did you have initial hesitations about him?"

"I did."

"And they never left you, did they?"

"No, they did not."

"But it took you almost seven years to finally fire him, correct?"

Sam responded is if he was in the moment and Webster was standing in front of his outstretched, pointed finger. "He was one of the most assful persons I have ever met—perhaps *the* most assful."

Doc continued, "In a letter to your brother, Orion, you wrote that you had never hated anyone as much as you hated him, didn't you?"

By this time, Sam was in a rage, reliving the utter financial collapse of his finances at the hands of Charles L. Webster, his niece's untrustworthy husband. He began sobbing.

We all gave him his moment of grief.

Doc handed Sam a piece of paper with a complete list of the financial failings that had plagued the Clemens family and sent them into hiding. "This list is your rain check. With it, you will change the finances of your family, Sam."

Sam looked up, took the piece of paper, read it briefly, then folded it up and placed it in his inside, right suit coat pocket. He wiped the remaining tears from his eyes, cheeks, and moustache, then looked up at Lou, Doc, Captain Backus, and me. "As I earlier asked, what becomes of my wife, my family, and me?"

Quickly, my three traveling companions turned toward me, defaulting, I suppose, to their *religious* friend.

Twain could tell that his questions had been deflected to me. He asked again, "Well, Arthur, are you prepared to tell me?"

Flinching at the first name he thought was mine, I leaned toward him. The urban robins of the Vienna woods broke the silence of the moment, singing just outside the apartment.

I let the moment linger and then responded. "Sam, you're all going to die." I paused again, waiting five seconds, and then added, "And so are we."

He jerked his head, pulling the half-smoked cigar from his lips. "What?"

I continued, "Sam, the nature of physics and all that we've laid out for you does not reduce the reality of life, death, and afterlife."

Sam responded in pensive silence. I continued.

"When you died in the other dimension means very little, just as it means very little here. What matters is what comes next." Without missing a beat, I added, "You believe in spiritualism and science, don't you?"

Twain took a puff from his cigar and nodded yes.

"And you've now seen that science is interconnected with creation, correct?"

Again, a nod.

"So creation itself demands a more meaningful nod to its author, doesn't it? I mean, look at it this way: *Tom Sawyer* didn't write itself."

This question received two puffs and a nod.

I said, "The three basic questions of humankind lay on the table every day for each of us to review or ignore."

Twain interrupted, "The three basic questions?"

"Yes. How did we get here? Why are we here? Where are we going?"

"Clever turn of the phrases," Sam acknowledged with a slight smile.

This time, I nodded.

"Sam, you've heard from Doc about the science of what the three of us have experienced with spacetime travel. You now know that we came specifically to see you. We need help with a plan. I'll unveil that in a bit. But right now, may I take just a few minutes to lace together the two strands of Isaac Newton's world for you?"

Sam extended his legs onto a spare kitchen table chair and crossed them, as one does when about to listen to a story. I could detect an openness and respect toward me as he withdrew the cigar from his lips with his left hand and motioned in slight circles, as if to say, "Continue."

I looked over at Doc, Lou, and the Captain and, I suppose, vulnerably asked, "Would you mind if I took just a small amount of time to address this updated version of the ghost in the machine?" They agreed that I should continue.

I turned to all of them.

"Friends, the five of us are witnesses to something larger than life, maybe larger than death and certainly on a plane with eternal life. Thank you, Doc, for allowing me to see that Isaac Newton focused his incredible brilliance on all things physical. Kudos to those who discovered his personal writings, or I should say will *rediscover* his personal writings on faith in 1936. Newton's mathematical mind has allowed us to see the creator behind the creation. His way of beginning the process of looking at life in science was improved upon by others, including you, Dr. Gersema." I motioned to Doc with respect.

He smiled, as I'd imagine a professor might smile when listening to his student's graduate thesis.

I slowly began. "We have the opportunity of changing lives and saving lives, millions of lives. At our disposal are tools that if used correctly can and will change the actions (and reactions) of men and women in history." I paused for a final sip of Livy Clemens's sweet lemonade.

"Sam, I know you are forcefully against anti-Semites and Vienna is full of those types both now and into the next three decades. Hitler and those at Café Central in January 1913 are simply the tip of the bloody knife held in the hand of this terrible worldview. Your opinion writings have been, and should continue to be, cleverly worded works that insult those needing to be insulted and tear apart the arguments of weak-minded fools. And yet there's more you can do through your humor and your writing. I'll explain."

Sam's raised eyebrows joined the upturned corners of his lips as he leaned forward.

"Doc and Lou, your passion to save your grandfathers, their families, and so many other Jewish families from their future fate under the Nazi regime motivate you. Doc, you were so motivated that you killed Hitler. And then we saw how much more terrible it could get. Your brilliance in science is being hamstrung by your unwillingness to consider Newton's most important comments—those of God."

Doc's eye's glistened. He looked down. Lou kept eye contact with me.

I turned my attention to Orrin Backus. "Captain, you are an eyewitness to the wholesale slaughter of countrymen killing one another in America during this hellacious uncivil war. You've seen the strategic significance of saving one man's life by what you and I did together to save General Sedgwick, correct?"

The Captain responded, "Yes."

"And you had parents who, though not scientists or intellectuals, were nonetheless clear in how they raised you. Do you remember their earliest teachings for you?"

He pursed his lips, looked off to the right corner of his eyes, and then fastened his glance directly onto my face.

"I do."

"What were they?" I asked.

"Father and Mother would begin every dinner meal with a statement, not so much a blessing, as some would know it, but a saying of sorts."

His present merged with his past. He was with us at Sam's kitchen table just months before the twentieth century was to dawn, but his mind and spirit were in the 1820s as he recalled sitting with his sister and brother before a family dinner.

"Father would always declare, 'The chief end of man is to glorify God and enjoy him forever.' We would all be silent for a moment or two until Mother closed our prayer with a gentle 'So be it?' and we children would respond, 'Amen.' I never knew where it came from; we just said it, and, I suppose, as members of our household, we believed it."

It was my time for wet eyes.

All of us could feel the imprint of two faithful parents on this faithful man, years later and a century later on these others.

I said, "Which brings us therefore to this crossroad, one that I submit to all of us in order to continue."

I paused and realized I was including Sam Clemens in our troop of traveling adventurers without his permission. "Including you, Sam, if you would like to join us for a short bit before we return you to your new opportunities in the past and then in your future."

He took a long final draw off his cigar stub and slowly exhaled, rubbing out the remnant of his enjoyment in a well-used ashtray. "Well, Arthur, you wrote your book. What did you call it?"

"*How to Steal a Pen Name and Make Lots of Money*," I responded without cracking a smile.

"Oh, that's rich!" Sam guffawed and slapped his knee, smiling the widest grin any of us had yet seen by him.

"Actually, it's called *A Change of Time*, about a series of daring adventures."

Sam responded, "I wrote a couple of books about some daring adventures; you might have read them."

We all chuckled knowingly.

He continued, "So it'd be pretty cowardly of me to remain in this decade, in this country, in these times of chaos and not move forward to make the future better for myself, my family, and the world, wouldn't it? If I didn't join you, Tom, Huck, and Becky might not take much of a shining to me, would they?"

It was our time to laugh.

"Okay." I nodded. "Friends, allow me to present to you how I think we must proceed."

We gathered together, and I presented my plan.

15

1913

Sam's hair seemed to get wilder as he stayed in Vienna but returned with us into the future via TC1 to January 1913. The momentary rush of spacetime travel brought a wide smile to his lips. It's what I'd always imagined old-time carriage enthusiasts showed the first time they saw a horseless carriage pass by, at what they called a breakneck speed.

"Now that was mixing a couple of rosy antifogmatics!" Sam howled, standing erect in his signature pure white suit jacket and slacks.

The Captain replied, "The dancin's gonna commence at early candle-lightin'." Both men nodded their heads, laughing, knowing exactly what they meant.

Doc and I shook our heads. He looked at me. "I'm not jiggy with those words, but I think they're glad to be here."

"Jiggy? I'm impressed, Doctor. Looks like you'll soon be dragging them into the late 1990s."

After getting settled in, I asked Sam and the Captain to recount the course of action we set in motion back at Mark Twain's Austrian residence.

The newest member of our group took the initiative. "I want to say something before we begin. The truth is I just can't believe that in all of my success for forty years as a writer and speaker, I have been deteriorating in my character. Reading that future piece you gave me, Doc—the one I'm supposed to pen in the next year, *Conversation with Satan*—I simply can't believe that's in me. It's a horrendous and hopeless piece about man and God. It's so dark. And people think that piece is what started me back from my career slump? God help me."

We all nodded and acknowledged his budding self-discovery. I said, "Indeed."

Sam smiled wryly at me.

He said, "To be clever, witty, and brooding at the expense of joy, humor, and hope is like writing all one's songs with discordant notes and hoping people will smile. Now they might smile—but only once the music stops."

Doc walked over to the Edison phonograph. "Agreed, Sam. Case in point," he remarked as he sorted through his revised series of music discs and read the title from one, a bootlegged copy of a song. "It's called 'When I'm Sixty-Two.'"

I said, "Don't you mean 'Sixty-Four'?"

Doc chuckled. "Apparently not to John, Pete, George, and Ringo." And he played the music on the Edison phonograph. Sam sat and listened to the music and lyrics, which were different from the lyrics I knew yet still quite clever.

As the song ended, Sam looked up and said, "Exactly my point. No discordant notes." And then he added, "I like that quartet."

I smiled and thought, *I suppose at sixty-two, Twain—and even Hemingway—could both use some joy and encouragement from the Beatles.*

"Okay, Sam, thank you," I said as we changed directions. "You and the Captain please summarize what we discussed in your house."

Sam was clear and cogent as he read from some small cards. "We are going to take a two-pronged strategy—a pincer movement—to gain a clear understanding of what these particular men believe and then challenge their involvement in this insidious anti-Semitic movement in Vienna. Doc, Lou, and Captain Backus will deal with three of the group, one at a time, at Café Central."

Doc elaborated, saying, "Stalin, Lenin, and Tito."

Sam responded, "Yes, those fellows." He paused, shuffling through the cards. "Arthur and I will use my celebrity and meet Hitler by first inviting Putzi to join us at the Café. None of these men will have met one another. Oh, and we'll all stay away from that one fellow ..."

"Trotsky," Doc said.

"Yes, Trotsky. He's a lost cause by this point," Sam stated.

"And the goals are clear," the Captain said. "We want to use what we collectively know about these men and challenge them to look at their futures differently."

"Agreed," Doc responded. "But not only that. These are men of passion and drive, men who have attached themselves to worldviews—or at least budding worldviews. They involve power and personal security and in some cases a lust for power and personal pain for others who do not agree with them."

Twain pulled a couple of cigars from the inside pocket of his white coat jacket and offered them to us, even to Lou. Doc alone accepted.

"If they were characters in one of my books," Sam said, "they'd be blackards." He and Doc used a bullet punch cutter on the ends of their cigars and then lit each up. The small blue clouds of smoke began to envelope us.

Sam continued, "Blackards, one and all—some redeemable, some not. And the key is to determine who fits where. That Trotsky is so deeply enmeshed in his belief system that he's always recruiting and never reflecting."

Sam shook his head, as if wondering how we would accomplish this effort. We all realized the costs if we failed. Millions of lives hung in the balance. WWI and WWII lay just in front of us.

Doc brought it in for a landing. "We need to determine if these men can be rescued from their debilitating worldviews and therefore, by default, change the world—a world they are moving toward the brink of disaster. If so, we do what we can at this moment in time and see the results that issue forth from our efforts. These are the plans we must pursue."

Sensing the intensity of the moment, Sam asked, "Or?"

"Or we all live the life you have lived these past forty years of cynicism and fear."

"Fear?"

"Yes, fear of loss, fear of growing older, fear of death."

We all paused. Sam took a draw on his cigar, tilted his head toward the ceiling, and exhaled.

"That's about where I've been," Sam concluded. "I've contributed to the sadness and downtrodden nature of hopelessness, making it seem funny but only at the expense of hope.

"My dear friends, that's about where the world has been." He paused and then said, "We may not be successful in changing the world, but we may just change ourselves and, by that, change *our* worlds."

I said, "There's an old Jewish proverb that says, 'The mind of man makes his plans.'"

The Captain said, "I remember that from my parents, and I believe there's a second part to it."

Surprised, I asked him if he knew what it was. He did not.

"But God directs his steps," Lou stated. "Maybe even *her* steps too?"

We all nodded in agreement.

A very big plan was suddenly unveiling itself, in very small steps.

16

1913

Sitting in an elegant booth in Vienna's Café Central, I suddenly looked up and saw six-foot-four Ernst F. Sedgwick "Putzi" Hanfstaengl as he strode in the front door on a sunny yet wintry January morning, in a most imposing yet elegant fashion. He carried a delicate card of invitation to meet the noted American humorist Mark Twain. Such cards were the norm in 1913 for inviting guests to meals and meetings. Telephones were rare at that time, so these cards were critical to the social order of proper Viennese society.

Sam and I were in a booth off to the left and halfway through the café near the second station of waiters. It gave us a vantage point to see the entire café at a single glance.

Having read Putzi's book, both of us were at a great advantage in understanding the twenty-five-year-old version of Herr Hanfstaengl. Having graduated from Harvard in 1909, Putzi moved to New York City and assumed management of the US branch of his family's art business, the Franz Hanfstaengl Fine Arts Publishing House. Their client list for photographs included three German kaisers—as well as Wagner, Liszt, Ibsen, and many other artists. His parents were friends of Mark Twain, the book stated.

"More like acquaintances," Sam muttered when I referred to that section. "Arthur, when I became famous, every person I ever met became my 'friend,' especially as they'd speak of me to others."

"Well, Sam, I wouldn't know about that. My books don't yet have the grasp yours do."

"Maybe that's so, but none of my books crease space and time like that little book of yours does." He patted his suit coat pockets once again but to no avail. "I've got it in here, somewhere," he mumbled. "Wait, I must have left it next to that little Hitler book back at the flat."

Doc and I looked at Sam. Doc said, "No, neither one of the books are back at the flat. I could not easily lay my hands on them as we got ready to come here."

Sam flatly said, "Well, we're going to have to go off our memories about them during this meeting."

That would not be difficult.

In fact, what caught my mind in "that little Hitler book," as Sam called it, were Putzi's frequent trips back and forth over the Atlantic, combined with his close friendships with former US president Teddy Roosevelt, William Randolph Hearst, Charlie Chaplin, and rising young New York state senator Franklin Roosevelt, making him a much sought-after cultural ambassador between Germany and America.

His literary friends included T. S. Elliot, Walter Lippman, John Reed, and Robert Benchley. Like his father, he was often described as "spectacularly handsome" and also like his father was rumored to have broken up many influential marriages.

Sam turned to me. "I *did* meet young Putzi in Berlin in 1891, I believe, when he was just under five years old. He was a little piggy boy, always eating things off our plates and off the serving tables. We were in Berlin with my cousin, Frau Greneralin von Versen, at a ball she was hosting. As I remember it, Putzi's mother and father were acquaintances of our family, and they brought this little chubby cherub to the party. I remember it for two reasons; that little tyke stayed up until two in the morning playing the piano for the assembled guests, and I got sick that night with the influenza and lung congestion. He played well, far as I can remember, through the echo of my head in the toilet bowl."

"Well, those are two very good reasons to recall the night," I mentioned, poking him as I saw Putzi walk toward us, hands outstretched.

"There he is, Mr. Mark Twain," Putzi said loud enough for those around us to hear and turn their necks toward us. "Welcomen nach Oestetrich."

Sam exited the booth, stood as erect as he could, seeming though to shrink as he stood next to this near giant of a man. "Allow me to introduce you to my friend, Arthur Peter Frampton," he said, remembering well the story of our sideline trip to Liverpool and blending it with his cheeky sense of humor. "He's a musician and an author," Sam added.

Putzi's eyebrows shot up. "Very nice to meet you, Herr Frampton. I too am a musician; maybe one day I'll be an author as well." His comment was that of a gentleman, expected to say such nice and proper things, though without any chance of us playing music together ever becoming a reality.

"Possibly," I coolly responded, nodding as he joined us in our booth.

"Herr Twain, how has our lovely Vienna been treating you?"

"It's always beautiful here, as though I've gone back in time." He looked at me and then added, "Or forward."

Putzi smiled an unknowing grin and continued on. "Mein Mutti und Papa remember you well as a friend of our family from the days in Berlin." I couldn't help but think he was saying this to add support to his own family's fictional legacy that overstated their relationship with this internationally known author.

"Uh huh," is all Sam contributed.

"Thank you so much for your kind invitation to renew our friendship after so many years. How old was I when we last met? Ten, fifteen years old?" He didn't actually expect Sam to answer, as his inflated and inaccurate prating continued unabated. For his part, Sam simply smiled his broad grin under the lip of his large white moustache.

"Und now we are at zis café. How may I serve you?"

Gunther was again our waiter, gentile as always, silently interrupting our conversation to receive the order for pastries, cakes, coffees, and the lone luscious dark chocolate, served hot in a delicate cup. His daughter Frieda had lost her front right tooth since they last served us, and the gap was cute for a little girl her age.

I began by saying, "May I call you Putzi?"

He looked surprised that in a formal setting, under such formal speech etiquette as the German language dictates, I would ask such an informal question of him. Maybe it was his youthful age reacting to a childhood baby name. Maybe it was that he was half-American and he was used to such immediate informality, but he acquiesced just the same and nodded yes.

"On behalf of Mr. Twain, I'm about to share a tale that is unbelievable. It involves you, your family member American General John Sedgwick, another man I'd like to introduce you to named Adolf Hitler, and a way of life that you will hardly comprehend, let alone accept. But it is enough to say that Mr. Twain needs your help."

"Absolutely. Anything for you, Herr Twain." Gunther set our order down, and Putzi dug into the pastry dish with zeal. Sam looked at me and smiled.

I continued, "The story as it is currently written involves you and Herr Hitler … in the future. It also involves your uncle John Sedgwick in the past."

Putzi turned his head toward me slowly.

"What?"

"As I said, it is a tale that will surprise you beyond anything you could dream up or believe, but it's true."

"You mentioned 'as it is currently written.' Who wrote it?" he asked as he followed a large slurp of espresso with an enormous bite of pastry.

Sam and I looked at each other, knowing this was the moment of unveiling.

"You did, forty years from now," I said.

He spewed his coffee and pastry all over Mark Twain's beautiful white suit.

17

1948

Christmas 1948 in Vienna was slightly snowy; the temperature was thirty-two degrees Fahrenheit. Snow was deepest in the Vienna Woods just northwest of the city, but Vienna itself was only mildly impacted by the snow.

It was a season of repair. The city had barely survived the bombings of WWII, with 20 percent of the city laid to waste after fifty-plus Allied bombing raids during a period of thirty-two months. Eighty thousand homes were destroyed, and many thousands of businesses were bombed or burned. Buildings were only now being rebuilt.

Café Central did not escape the citywide destruction either. Partially bombed, it would remain closed for three decades until it was remodeled.

So, as postgraduate student and spacetime traveler Lou Abraham walked toward it, through the streets of Vienna during this Christmas season, she was unnerved. The beauty of Café Central was in partial ruins, certainly, but that wasn't what made her nervous.

Without permission, she had taken two books: Putzi's and mine. She placed her hand on the DNA on Putzi's book and arrived thirty-five years into the future. In her curiosity of wondering what she would be like as Louise—a woman in her midfifties—this twenty-two-year-old version of herself traveled to the only place she could think of that would allow her a peek at her older self: Vienna, Austria.

And now she felt like a fool. There was no place to possibly meet her older self.

There seemed no place for the young version of Lou to figure out how Putzi's autobiography would have been published in 1957 and then given by her to some man during Christmas in 1948, nine years before the publication.

Lou glided past the undead remains of Café Central. She was almost equally ghostly in her otherworldly walking, muscle memory taking over as she turned this way and then that. Within a handful of minutes, she was standing in front of what she recognized had been Dr. Russell Gersema's first-floor flat. "There's no way he could be here," she said to herself, hoping that she was wrong.

Her ringing of the doorbell went unanswered. The name tag listed the occupant's identity as Beatrice Schubert. The flat's exterior had aged, as war had done to all who lived through it. The snow began to fall. She stood hopeless and felt foolish— the vanity of youth mingled with the curiosity on which each of us would act, if given the chance. She had no place to go, no knowledge of how to return to this very flat in 1913, no experience in the proper use of TC1. Yet she was smart and had to think her way out of this spacetime dilemma. She stood immobile, thinking, retracing what she had observed as she had watched Doc and me as we traveled.

Then she looked down. There at her feet, the small stoop of steps was awash in blue ice melt. As the snowflakes fell to the ground, her hopes began to soar. Lou thought again. She opened the signed copy of *Hitler: The Missing Years* and turned to her own handwriting and read out loud, "'Putzi Hanfstaengle—a friend of

Beatrice Schubert's—and hence was briefly, as it were, just a step removed from the nefarious Hitler. How time passes!'"

She turned again to the flat's door, disregarding the apparent broken doorbell, and rapped firmly on the door itself with five knocks, singsong-saying, "Shave and a haircut ..."

The door opened, and a very pretty, professional, middle-aged American woman responded, "Shave and a haircut? Two bits." The two women looked at each other. The guest was surprised at how familiar the host looked, and the host was surprised at how young and naïve the guest at her doorway appeared.

"Hello, Lou. I've been expecting you."

It was Louise Abraham.

Lou fell onto the fainting couch, unconscious.

1913

The temporary lack of possession by us of the key books, *Hitler: The Missing Years* and *A Change of Time*, left Sam and me in a precarious position while we explained the story to Putzi. The presence of Mark Twain was the only redeeming truth for this tall, elegant, and young international businessman. I allowed Sam to lay out the story, the plot points that had happened, and the character of the protagonists and antagonists, as only Mark Twain could. His wit was sharp; his hope was alive.

Putzi responded, "So, you're telling me that I will befriend an Austrian named Adolf Hisler ..."

"Hitler, Adolf Hitler," I corrected him.

"Hitler, an itinerant former art school reject who will leave Vienna, secure political and military power within Germany, soon bringing Western civilization to its knees?" The look on his face was indescribable.

Sam blew out one of his celebrated bellows of cigar smoke and simply said, "Veritas."

Putzi, catching the reference to Harvard's motto, responded, "And what proof do I even have that you, Dr. Gersema, are from the future and that you, Mark Twain, are from the past?"

Thinking quickly and acting with resolve, Sam asked Putzi what his favorite three Mark Twain quotes were. Putzi responded with the first two quotes that came to his mind. "'The secret of getting ahead is getting started.'" He paused and then added the next one, "'If you tell the truth, you don't have to remember anything.'"

Sam jumped in. "Not 'The report of my death was an exaggeration'?"

Putzi said, "Of course that is everyone's favorite."

Then I saw the genius of Samuel Clemens exhibit itself.

Sam leaned across the table, looked directly into Putzi's eyes, and said, "Do you know when I wrote that quote about my supposed death?"

Putzi cocked his head and guessed, "When I was a boy."

Sam nodded. "Yes, in 1897 in London. And do you remember what actually happened in 1910?"

Putzi's eyes grew from an interested focus to confusion to utter disbelief. Two words barely escaped from his lips as he pushed up into the back of the booth, scared, as if to escape.

"You ... died."

Sam smiled and took a long drag from the remnant of his final cigar, stubbing it out into the ashtray and releasing the final gust of wind from his lungs that carried the blue smoke toward the ceiling.

"Apparently, the report is still an exaggeration."

Lou had put us in an untenable position. Without either of the autographed copies of Putzi's or my book, we were truly 'strangers in a strange land,' as her Torah referred to its main characters, Moses and Joshua. Nothing could transport Doc, Sam, the Captain, and me to either Putzi's world *or* my world. We four were stuck in a sort of cold dimensional desert, in January 1913, sitting in Doc's flat in Vienna.

The meeting with Putzi at Café Central had gone as well as could be hoped, despite Sam's white suit being stained with coffee and the remnants of an Austrian tart. Putzi peppered Sam about his father and mother, their meeting in Berlin, his own appearance as a five-year-old boy, and so on. He seemed to want to know that sitting before him really was Mark Twain, even though he'd suddenly remembered the news of Samuel L. Clemens's passing that happened three years before in 1910. I found it extremely ironic that Sam's premature death in 1897 had matured in 1913 and still had a measure of humor to it.

With Doc's residential address in hand, Putzi agreed to meet later in the day at four in the afternoon in our flat to further discuss the possibilities of meeting "this Hitler tramp," as the cultured German began calling him. Putzi's parting words were simple, "My one desire is to live long enough to see a Germany, and indeed a world, where these Hitlers are no longer possible." We would one day see these words in print.

Doc reported back that he and the Captain had been unsuccessful in their attempts to ingratiate themselves with Lenin, Stalin, and Tito. Doc seemed tired and unsure of the next steps. Had Lou been with them, as originally planned, she might have added much to the discussion. But she had abandoned them.

Captain Orrin Backus was quite clear in his observations of his assigned *personnel projects*. "I'm not sure if it was my American accent or whether they could read my opinions of each of them, but it did not work. The cold European shoulder of disinterest was turned my Yankee way." Pivoting to Sam, the Captain smirked and said, "Well, you might have been closer than you thought when you wrote your Connecticut Yankee, Hank Morgan, was almost burned at the stake by the Europeans."

Sam nodded. "We never did see Hitler at the café. And I suppose burning at the stake is a cleaner demise than being vomited to death by Putzi!" The two riverboat pilots laughed, the sort of thing we *all* needed at this moment.

Doc took the lead in the discussion. "Even with Lou having taken the two books, we still have some alternatives. To begin with, we possess volume 2 of Grant's memoirs, and we have documents written by you, Sam. The DNA from these two sources along with TC1 will help us return to those time slots."

Sam interrupted, "But for what reason? Even if Hitler did not yet show, we're attempting to make the connection between Putzi and Hitler successful. We should all stay together, waiting for Lou to return. We're all faced with the dilemma of Newton's summary that the world as we know it will end in 2060. We must do what we can to stop that." I had not seen Sam Clemens this serious.

The Captain said, "We certainly could do that. Also, we made the successful effort to keep General Sedgwick alive, apparently shortening the length of the Civil War. And ultimately, we need to flush out Lafayette."

Dr. Russ Gersema's body language seemed to agree with the two men yet signal something else, something of a new direction. He sat with his legs elegantly crossed, slowly flicking lint off his pant legs, as was his custom when he was entering into a deeper thought, leading to a discussion.

"Gentlemen, do I have permission to speak freely to the three of you?" We each nodded our approval.

"Very well," he responded as he stood. We were again his students, and his recitation voice stated simply, "Let us begin."

The professor walked over to the Edison phonograph and placed a disc on it. As the record crackled, he asked, "When is the life we know … gone?" All of us were quiet.

He continued, "Listen and then we'll talk about it." It was the Beatles, sans Paul. The lead vocal on it was Pete Best. It was a song I had never before heard, titled "Gone."

Gone!
We should be laughing at the fools that tried to
find us
But the rules can never last
Gone!
We should be dancing in the street
How many ways can we be freed from what is
past?
How long is forever, is forever

Doc let the song complete itself and then removed the disc from the Edison machine and pointed directly at me. "The melody and lyrics are haunting, not just because the world in which we once lived was impacted by a music group from Liverpool—even a revised version of the group—but because the principle of being gone in all of our worlds is always present."

Rather than allowing any sadness to envelop us, Doc smiled; it ignited our responses and our smiles like a struck match.

He continued, "Dimensional spacetime travel has shown each of us some remarkable changes in the lives of those we touch or will touch."

He turned to Orrin Backus. "Captain, you have seen what futuristic writers like Edward Bellamy and Aldous Huxley only wished they could have seen. You were plucked out of your Ohio business duties to serve in the War of the Rebellion. Then, your wartime duties as a riverboat pilot for the Northern Armies were thrust on you, and you did your duty. Because of that duty and the purchase of U. S. Grant's memoirs, I invited you to Vienna, Austria. You've seen what is possible for good with your own eyes—and, because of your brother, what is very bad. You've been with us, helping us in waters through which only a riverboat pilot could navigate."

The Captain smiled and accepted the kind words of affirmation. Doc turned to Sam.

"And, Sam, you have seen far more than what your still-vivid Connecticut Yankee imagination could ever dream up. You have now lived your own Hank Morgan life. I have seen joy come into your eyes, I've experienced love and hope emanate from you during this phase of our experience together. I've seen and heard your humor as genuine and not as a mask for pain. Mark Twain needed this."

It was the only time I had seen my friend Sam tear up. He simply leaned his elbows onto his knees and looked down at the ground.

Doc continued, "And, Author, you were selected to join me as a man of faith with keen perception, an author keeping track of this storyline and keeping us on track for what we each have had to accomplish. You didn't disappoint me as we walked together."

I was beginning to think that Doc was dismissing the three of us and then dispatching us back to our pre-spacetime travel lives; I was partially correct.

He continued speaking to me. "And, Author, I need you to keep helping me move forward."

He paused and smiled as though he had an unexpected gift for both of the other men … because he did. He handed each a single rolled-up small sheet of paper with pen writing on it. Doc looked like an academic handing out small diplomas.

"Orrin and Sam, your services are no longer required by me."

Both men looked crestfallen and confused and began to protest. Doc cut them off.

"Gentlemen, each of you has in his possession sheets of paper with facts penned on them that pertain only to you. They are bullet points from me to you regarding what you can choose to do as you enter back into your lives."

Both men unfurled their sheets and began to look at the bullet points.

Sam spoke up first, quoting an unusual item. "'When you arrive in the Sandwich Islands, buy tracks of land near and on the beach in each island you reside. Have them deeded to you and Olivia Clemens, even though you and she will not have yet met when the purchase happens.'" Sam looked up. "I, I, I uh …"

Doc pointed to the paper as if to demand that Sam read the next bullet point, which he obediently did.

"'Do not invest in a publishing company of your own or into printing inventions. Do not hire a man named Charles L. Webster for anything *ever*.'"

There were eleven or twelve more bullet points on the paper, each with a similar admonition for the owner to read and consider.

Sam slapped the paper with the back of his knuckles and said, "Well, I *know* this already. I should have already done or not done these things in the past. How is it going to help me *now and in the future*?"

It was Doc's time to wear the smug Mark Twain smile, one worn when writing his or her story without an audience yet knowing the plot twists.

While reaching into his file on the desk, withdrawing a single letter dated 1866 from Hawaii, signed by Mark Twain, Doc began to read:

Reflections

As we came in sight we fired a gun, and a good part of Honolulu turned out to welcome the steamer. It was Sunday morning, and about church time, and we steamed through the narrow channel to the music of six different church bells, which sent their mellow tones far and wide, over hills and valleys, which were peopled by naked, savage, thundering barbarians only fifty years ago! Six Christian churches within five miles of the ruins of a pagan temple, where human sacrifices were daily offered up to hideous idols in

the last century! We were within pistol shot of one
of a group of islands whose ferocious inhabitants
closed in upon the doomed and helpless Captain
Cook and murdered him, eighty-seven years ago;
and lo! their descendants were at church! Behold
what the missionaries have wrought!

Sam smiled. "Where did you get that old letter?"

Doc replied, "I collect signatures." Both men smiled.

I opened the cabinet and retrieved some small bottles of Coca-
Cola and said, "You just might need some refreshment before you
depart."

Sam pulled me aside for a private conversation. "Arthur, every
time someone mentions your name, you flinch. Why is that?"

Orrin was listening in, moving closer to the Coke bottles as I
was opening them.

"Well …" I paused, then realized how he might best
understand my dilemma. "Sam, just as you somehow stumbled
onto your own pen name, my name was sort of forced on me. I'm
not Author, or Arthur, or Peter Frampton. I'm …"

"Shush," he said, holding his finger to his lips. He leaned
toward me. "Whisper it."

Orrin leaned into hear as well.

I whispered my name. Sam smiled, nodded his head, and had
a certain gleam in his eyes. "May I see that pen?"

I handed it to him, and he wrote something on another small
piece of paper he was holding.

After he was done speaking to me, we both turned back to the
group, finishing our Cokes.

The plan was set. Sam Clemens would repeat his life having
no memory of these days, only having that sheet as well as the
sheet he had earlier received, listing all his failures. It was now
his time of choosing to see the world as it could be and smiling,
rather than mocking the world as it was.

Oh, and he might just become, *and stay,* wealthy, helping others and touching many more lives in what would be his new joyful life of writing than he did through his pain.

Orrin, Doc, and I each gave affectionate hugs to Sam as he securely held onto the letter. In moments, he released his grip on us and stepped onto telluric current number one.

Mark Twain was gone.

Fluttering to the floor as he disappeared was a small slip of paper with fresh ink on it, ripped as it were from the backside of an envelope. I picked it up from the floor. On it was written, "You changed my life. I *will* change yours. Sam 'Mark Twain' Clemens."

Doc and I smiled as we turned to Orrin.

I couldn't resist. "Contestant number two ..."

The Captain looked at me quizzically, and Doc saved us from another awkward spacetime moment. "Never mind, Captain. Just unfurl your note and let me know if you have questions."

The Captain read all the bullet points, making not a single reaction or response until the end. Scrunching his eyes, he looked at Doc and said, "What in the world is Hollywood?"

I laughed and looked at Doc.

Dr. Gersema, global spacetime traveler, apparent Hawaii real estate provocateur, and now entertainment producer, didn't miss a beat. He pointed at the bullet points on the Captain's paper.

"Orrin, you'll return to Ohio from the Civil War and lead a good life. At a certain time, you will follow your son to Southern California and build a very large company by founding the citrus industry, as well as the grape industry. You will find the areas of San Bernardino and Riverside to be to your liking and will want to settle there. But do not limit your real estate holdings to only those areas. Keep moving toward the beaches of Los Angeles and buy as much land as you can in what will be billed as Hollywoodland. Buy land along the foothills, moving into the mountains. Understand?"

Orrin responded, "But a man can't plant and harvest easily on slopes."

Doc poked the paper and laughingly stated, "Pretend my written directions are the boundaries of a river route, Captain, penned by one who went before you and mapped it out himself."

Orrin understood. He then asked if he might borrow a pen. I grabbed one and handed it to him as he opened up volume 2 of U. S. Grant's personal memoirs. He opened the first page and wrote something next to his original signature, which I could not make out.

I looked at Captain Orrin Backus, the man who had originally owned my two-volume set, a very valuable and deeply important gift from my bride. "Orrin, my late wife, blessed me with those books many years ago. Many years in the future, you will give them up. I'm very glad. Because of that gift, I now have the gift of your friendship. Thank you. Travel well with it. I'll get it back in due time."

The Captain's laugh lines—what were called *horvats* by some in his day—curled upward around his eyes. "In due time, indeed. Thank you," he said to Doc and me.

The self-acclaimed "independent" religious riverboat captain, future SoCal land baron, and soon-to-be Civil War veteran turned to me and said, "As my mother and father said to me—and you have shown me by your actions—I say to you: the chief end of man is to glorify God and to enjoy Him forever."

With that, he opened the book, placed his hand on the signature, and stepped onto TC1.

Pete Best's lyric echoed in me. Both friends were now gone.

18

1948

Lou later told me this ensuing story. I also asked her to jot down the specifics of this amazing event, an event that has never happened to another human being. I'll do my best to relate it to you here, from her notes.

As Lou revived, she looked around the flat, seeing exactly what she had seen before: the large sofa chairs, the bookshelves, the wallpaper, light fixtures, the butcher paper with charcoal writing on it.

Yet each item was a bit more tattered and less colorful than she recalled. The sofa stuffing of the fainting couch seemed flatter, the wallpaper darker, and the butcher paper writing less vivid. What people see as the degradation (or entropy, as physicists call the changes) had begun to occur by the movement of time.

Yet, as a postgraduate student in physics, Lou knew better than this. Newton's second law of thermodynamics says that everything tends toward high entropy. Nothing was degrading; rather, it should be realized as something connected to the amount of ways a system has to rearrange itself. Each time it does that, it's called a microstate of that same system. Things don't degenerate;

they simply try to find the max number of microstates. We look at it and see tattered wallpaper. In reality, energy is shifting in the same space.

Lou stood up and walked slowly around the library, unsure of how she arrived at the flat, unsure if it was 1948 yet sure that this was exactly where she had to be. Something about the butcher paper caught her eye. All the pages of papers were still hung where she remembered them, except one. All now had Scotch tape holding them in place, except one—that same newest one. Instead, it had the drippings of wax holding it up. On it were printed in Doc's handwriting three main points about something.

She looked over to where the Edison phonograph machine had been, and in its place was a Philco M-15 record player with various LP album covers by the Beatles scattered about. Lou picked up a couple and glanced at the titles: *The Casbah, Meet the Beatles, Captain Pepper's Lonely Hearts Club Band, Rubber Spirit, The Tan Album,* and a number of others—none of which meant much to Lou except that the albums were much bigger in size than what she had listened to on the Edison phonograph player. She was fascinated by the physics of capturing sound and replaying it on these machines.

A soothing female voice from behind her and by the doorway broke her concentration.

"Columbia Records forever changed the industry this year, 1948, when they evolved records from seventy-eight revolutions per minute to 33 1/3 rpms." She then paused to take inventory of her guest. "The vinyl records got better."

Lou turned to see the woman and recognized her as the one who met her at the front door. The one who caught her as she fainted was now carrying a cup of coffee toward Lou. She was lovely, and her eyes were kind. A small decorative cross hung loosely on a silver chain draped around her neck. Lou gave the cross a second look to make sure.

Lou was quiet, knowing who her host was but not knowing how the two of them were together and separate at the same time. Host and guest were the same person.

The host continued with technical small talk to soothe the guest's utter confusion. "Columbia's engineer Peter Goldmark began in '39, working on changing the 78 rpm toward a new standard. Though it could extend playback by up to twenty-plus minutes on each side, the history of 33 1/3 records failed due to heavy record player pick-ups that would cut through the vinyl after only a handful of plays. Customers were livid. But this year, they fixed the problem, and these new albums with better technology will change the world."

The host placed the cup of coffee on the table—coffee that already had the perfect amount of sugar and cream in it. "Just as you, uh we, like it," Louise Abraham said plainly.

Silence washed over the two of them as they sat across from each other, peering at each other, studying aspects of each's face and body as though looking at a four-dimensional mirror of themselves.

Lou looked at her. "Scientifically, how can this be?"

Louise responded, "We'll get to that. For right now, would you mind if I settle some other pressing items that must be dealt with?"

"Yes, go ahead."

"Lou, when you absented yourself from Doc, Arthur, Sam, and the Captain, you took the two books that were essential to them—Arthur's book and Putzi's book."

Lou looked down while saying, "I uh, just ... um, wanted ..."

Louise finished her sentence, "To see what *we* would look like in 1948. I know, I know. *And* it placed our friends in serious difficulties. As it was, Doc creatively figured out how to send Sam and Orrin back to their lives. And now they need Putzi's book and Arthur's book."

Ignoring the second part, Lou said, "What? They're gone?"

"Indeed they are, Lou. They went back to their lives, changed quite a few things in history as a result of their time with us, and in time passed away. Sam died in 1910; the Captain died earlier in 1898."

Lou could not contain her grief. She wept.

Louise patted her younger self's arm, then slowly went over to the record player and played an album of an artist, Bart Millard.

(It was a gift I had given Lou, far in the future, however that works! Bart Millard would not be born until 1972 and would in 1994 form a band called MercyMe.)

Louise chose the song titled "Dear Younger Me," sung by an older man to a younger version of himself.

The song played to both the women's shared hearts, though one lyric touched them deepest:

Dear younger me,
Do I give some speech about how to get the most out of your life
Or do I go deep?
And try to change the choices that you'll make,
Cuz they're choices that made me

Louise turned off the Philco record player and returned to her sofa chair. "Dear Lou, I've been waiting for you, knowing that your curiosity would lead you here in 1948, knowing that I would be the only one who could answer your questions and redirect you toward the things that matter most. Age doesn't matter, looks don't matter, and career doesn't matter—not in the long run."

Lou responded, "But how did you know I'd take the books and sneak out in the middle of the night, traveling through spacetime to see myself—never thinking that I'd actually meet myself!"

Louise cocked her head and arched an eyebrow as she looked over the tops of her reading glasses at Lou, "Dear younger me ... allow me to read you something from the works of Dr. Russell Gersema on his landmark account on spacetime travel and its future (or past) possibilities. It'll be published next century." Louise adjusted her glasses and read from the page in her hand.

"'When journeying through spacetime, it is vital that travelers keep a written form of communication open between dimensional silos so that in the unfortunate event of DNA being taken or compromised the travelers can still maintain communication—even if only one way—with those who are ahead of them in spacetime, while in the same silo.'"

Louise looked at Lou. "You want to return to 1913 and stand in this very flat with Doc and the Author, but you can't. The two books you have in your possession are focused on 1948 and later. Nothing about 1913. You cannot return backward."

Lou interrupted Louise in despair. "What a silly, foolish person I was. I took a one-way trip, and now I can't get back."

Louise looked at her younger self. "Your actions weren't foolish. You were just curious. In fact, isn't that what science demands that we be? Should you have received help from Doc? Of course. But that didn't happen, and here we are." Then Louise paused and smiled, adding, "Actually, I was looking forward to meeting my younger self. Who gets that chance in life to see how brilliant one actually is when younger?"

Both women laughed their particular deep-sounding yet soft chortles in unison, catching the harmony of their laughs, making them laugh even louder. They needed this chance for humor.

When Louise and Lou settled down, the younger asked the older, "Did you purposely sign Putzi's book with the intention of having me use it to make this side eddy of a trip in 1948? And who are Smith and Beatrice Schubert?"

Louise kindly answered the younger version of herself, "I bought Putzi's book shortly after it was published in 1957—"

Lou interrupted with a shout, "Nineteen fifty-seven? How old do I get?"

Without missing a beat, Louise quietly continued, "I traveled through spacetime into the future to Riverside, California, in 1977.

I signed the book and gave it to the owner of the store, Smith Brandenburg, a man I had never before met. I paid him cash for the Grant memoirs and had him attach Putzi's book to it—that the three books would now be a package deal and sold only to a woman, whose full name I gave him, who would shortly arrive seeking to buy the Grant set for her husband in honor of their wedding anniversary. I explained that Smith should feel no guilt at charging her the same high price I had just paid him, knowing that just such a deal would appeal to his profit-centered business mind."

All three books were together from then on, until Lafayette Backus stole volume 1.

As if an afterthought, Louise answered Lou's question about Beatrice Schubert. "Oh, that's just a name I made up and placed on the door knocker and in the book so you would connect the dots. Did you like the blue ice, by the way? Doc had a hundred-year-old bag he bought in the future and left in the closet. I chose it to ensure you'd know you were at the right spot." She seemed quite pleased with herself. Lou thought, *I would be too. Wait. I am … wait.* And then both women smiled the same smile.

Louise, however, caught motion in her peripheral vision and stopped smiling. She turned toward the one sheet of wax-adhered sticky corners. Lou's eyes followed her older self to the sheet with the three points from Doc on it.

Both women's mouths dropped open.

Lou and Louise saw a fourth point suddenly appear, with one small sentence being written upon it as they watched. It was in Doc's handwriting—written in this very room of Lou's past to her in this very room of Doc's future.

It was the communication link his previous paper had addressed, Louise realized.

"Come back. Use my DNA."

Lou and Louise watched as the handwriting from 1913 appeared on the butcher paper. Just as soon as the letters D-N-A were complete, Louise knew exactly what to do.

"Of course! We need to tear off that piece of paper right now and move," she said. She lunged at the paper, ripping it from the candle wax that held it to the wall. Lou joined her, clutching the two vital books that needed to be returned to the past, as they made it to the center of the room, examining just where the TC cut its swath across the floor.

Knowing that this was a rare moment in anyone's life to take an actual physical inventory of oneself, both women paused and looked at each other, as if standing before a mirror.

Louise simply said to Lou, "You are a beautiful, bright, and wonderful young woman. You are *already* a success. Walk in that truth. After all, you are made in God's image." Louise then took off the silver necklace with the cross, placed it gently in Lou's right palm, and closed Lou's fingers. Lou did not react.

The young lady looked at her older self and saw a joy in her eyes that she did not currently possess and dismissed the thought. Knowing also that it was her responsibility to return to us Putzi's book—and mine—to 1913, Lou said to her older self, "The previous trips were simple, right? How exactly did we do it?"

Louise saw the tendency in her younger self of *getting ready to get ready*—a problem with perfectionists.

"Just hold the paper, hold the books, and hold your breath," Louise shouted at her as she pushed her younger self onto TC1 and immediately into the past.

In an instant, Lou was gone.

In another instant, Lou was among us in the flat, holding two books and the sheet of paper that also hung on the wall. Also, in her right palm remained the cross and necklace. Doc clapped in relief and hugged Lou as she stumbled into the flat.

"I am so glad to see you, Lou. So glad you were wise and made your way to the flat."

Lou was embarrassed as much by Doc's exuberance as by the strong and meaningful hug he gave her.

"I thought you'd be furious with me for taking the books," Lou said.

"Are you serious? I was petrified that I might never see you again," he said and paused, noticing how public his admiration suddenly had become. "Anyway, you are here, and we have the books again." He glanced at his timepiece and announced, "It's almost four o'clock, and Putzi will be arriving here shortly."

Lou's perfectionism seemed to evidence itself still. She obviously feared that she'd deeply broken Doc's trust. He saw her hesitancy and reached for her again.

Bringing her to himself and seeming not to care that I was witnessing such rare personal warmth, Dr. Russell Gersema held Lou tightly and whispered something to her that I could not hear. Their hug was much more tender the second time. I blushed.

The polite knock at the door interrupted the moment. For me, it was thankful timing. I advanced to the entry.

Opening the heavy Victorian door, I said with a smile, "Putzi, what a pleasure to have you at Dr. Gersema's house." I extended my hand in greeting.

He seemed to have forgotten that we met just hours ago at Café Central and that he had suggested he and Peter Frampton should play music together. He was the type of man who only really remembered people who could help him. What could a musician named Peter Frampton ever do for him?

Every bit of the wealthy German aristocrat evidenced itself as he placed his coat and scarf over my outstretched arm. Saying nothing, he strode past me down the hallway.

He then spoke in a sort of singsong way, "Herr Gersema, wo bist du?"

"We're in the library," Doc responded.

I trailed slowly behind him, taking time to hang his coat and scarf on the hall tree. By the time I turned left and entered into the library, Putzi had already clicked his heels, shook hands with Doc, and was in the process of kissing the extended right hand of our brilliant and recently returned postgraduate student.

"Louise. What a lovely name, my dear." Putzi's charm was well practiced.

Doc looked clear-eyed at Putzi and invited him to be seated, which he accepted with great enthusiasm.

"Putzi, by your act of coming to my flat, it would appear that you take seriously the story we earlier presented to you, correct?"

Putzi took out a German cigarette from a golden case and tapped it twice against the side of his silver lighter, nodding his head in agreement. He lit the cigarette and blew the harsh cloud of tobacco smoke away from all the others but in the direction where I sat. "How could I not? You brought a dead man back to life. Mark Twain shook my hand three years after his death—his *real* death." Then he laughed oddly.

Doc dismissed the death comment as well as the laugh—for he knew both comments were spoken out of insecurity.

Looking around, Putzi asked, "Is Mr. Twain still here?"

Doc's crisp answer ended any additional questions regarding Sam. "No," Doc said flatly. "Further, what you are *most* interested in is your autobiography, correct?"

"Of course," the lanky, handsome young German replied. He was noticeably excited to see this supposed book.

Rather unceremoniously, Doc tossed *Hitler: The Missing Years* to its author for him to read for the first time.

The late afternoon moved quickly into evening as Putzi read his own words. He paused at one point, placing the book on his lap, covering his eyes with both palms, saying only, "Six million dead?" before bringing the book back into his line of sight and continuing.

By nine o'clock in the morning, Putzi finished the book. He looked up at Lou, Doc, and me and said with an exhausted spirit, "Extraordinary. The last line of this book is exactly how I feel at this moment." He reopened the book to its last page and read,

"'My one desire is to live long enough to see a Germany, and indeed a world, where Hitlers are no longer possible.'"

Doc looked first at Lou and then me. We both nodded. He turned to Putzi. "Are you with us?"

Putzi sighed the deepest of sighs and responded, "Yes. How could I not be, for God's sake." Something had happened to General Sedgwick's relative.

19

1913

Putzi listened to Doc and Louise (as she now asked to be called) without moving a single facial muscle. His autobiography lay on his lap.

"So, Putzi, if we can redirect Hitler away from politics and back toward art—even getting him accepted by the Fine Arts Academy Vienna—the world as you wrote it would change," Doc said flatly, without looking at me. The specter of Ernst Röhm hung over the conversation as I looked at Doc. He refused to return my glance.

Doc continued, "Putzi, when you were little and first in America, other than your father, who was the most central figure in your life?"

Putzi responded without any delay, "John Sedgwick was. He became general of the armies in the Civil War. He was vital to President Hamlin after Lincoln's impeachment and removal from office. Prospered as a businessman and statesman. Then he became president of the United States. He mentored John Hay and brought him aboard as vice president. Most historians credit him with having also brought the rebellion to a close in late '63. My uncle John was amazing."

I looked at Doc. He returned the shocked look and said almost in a whisper, "President Hamlin, Lincoln impeached, the Civil War ending two years earlier in 1863?"

I thought it best to not yet navigate those waters; I'd examine these new facts soon enough.

I turned to Louise. "For all of our sakes, allow me to clarify his remarks. His uncle John was indeed *the* General John Sedgwick, whose life I saved when I tackled him to the ground during the Battle of Spotsylvania Court House."

"Of course, of course," Putzi responded rather curtly, as if being bothered by a butler.

Doc continued, "So when your father passed away, Uncle John took you under his wing and helped you mature, correct?"

"Yes, he mentored me. In essence, he made me more American than German."

Nursing my bruised butler ego, I thought, *Uncle John should have tried a little harder.* But I shook it off and quickly reentered the conversation.

Louise said, "Putzi, it seems like you must have a soft spot for helping other people, just as was done for you."

"Well, if what you are suggesting is that I take Hitler under my wing, it seems as though I did that in the other dimension of spacetime, and look how this monster turned out." His body noticeably shivered as he spoke about the evil of Hitler.

He added, "We still have Ernst Röhm to worry about. From what I wrote, that man truly enjoyed hurting people. His Brownshirts were completely reprobate in their lives and in their use of perversion, terror, and death."

I looked directly at Doc and could not contain myself any longer. "Are you going to tell them or should I about our visit to Röhm's world as the Founder?"

For some reason, Doc tried to dismiss the severity of what we observed. His reluctance to enter into that discussion was palpable. He could tell I was not going to stay quiet.

"Go ahead and tell them," he said, almost as if he had been defeated.

I laid out the story in specific detail—the full facts about an American Reich that Louise had not heard before. Putzi was truly engaged in the tale, listening intently.

At the conclusion of the story's recital, Putzi paused and said to me, "For a butler, you really are an extraordinary storyteller. That was riveting. You must consider becoming an author."

I couldn't resist. "No, thanks. I'm happy being a musical butler."

I suggested we all take a break for refreshments and walk over to Café Central. They agreed.

As we walked the relatively short distance from the flat to the coffeehouse, Putzi was ahead of us, arm in arm with Louise, laughing and chatting. I pulled Doc closer to me and spoke softly.

"What is going on? Why are you intent on Putzi mentoring Adolf Hitler? Even if he does succeed at helping make Hitler an artist, we are stuck with Nazism. Are you *honestly* not aware of the deeper level of evil at play here?"

Doc slowed his pace even more, distancing us from Louise and Putzi. "Of course I am aware. When I killed Hitler, you and I both experienced the cascading evil—even to the level of having almost all Jews killed, including my family, my family's family, Jewish leaders and …" His voice went quiet. As if to regain some level of strength, he barked, "And Louise. I can't let her die—or worse, let her never be. I simply can't let her *not* be a part of my life. Maybe helping Hitler will somehow give me time to think about how to handle Röhm."

Having lost my own love, I understood his fear. Yet the picture was much bigger than one person or two budding lovers.

I said, "So how does letting Putzi mentor Hitler eliminate Ernst Röhm and what will surely be Röhm's—as Louise wrote— 'nefarious' retinue of crazed Nazis?"

We turned the corner in the neighborhood, heading toward the café.

"I'm not completely certain," Doc confessed, "but I do know that killing a person for what he or she is going to do in the future doesn't work in the present."

"You sound like me when we first started."

He nodded. "It seems I'm becoming more like you, Author."

"And I may be moving in your direction," I stated flatly.

"We've got to figure this out. I need time," he said. "How we deal with these incredibly evil leaders' insatiable appetite for power is key to cutting this Gordian knot."

We came to the straight path that leads up the right side to Café Central's beautiful triangle front entrance. I laughed to myself at the comment of needing time as we turned the corner for the final fifteen feet to the door. "Well, however we cut through the time knot, it's always best done with chocolate tarts and coffee, isn't it?"

Doc laughed and said, "And hot chocolate too, Author. Hot chocolate too."

20

January 18, 1913

Walking into the elegant entrance of Café Central is akin to finding oneself suddenly within the most strikingly beautiful interior photographs of the Victorian age. It's difficult to describe other than to say photographs never completely and accurately capture reality.

Nighttime in Vienna makes it even more gorgeous.

Twenty or so arched architectural trusses, painted gold and white, give a cathedral feeling to the café's ceiling. It's like attending a religious experience for foodies. The shared expression of the spirit is doled out one cake or cup at a time. It offers a communion of sorts for those who need temporary comfort in this world.

I tensed up as we entered. I noticed something at that moment I had not observed in past visits. The sheer volume of customers had increased. The place was packed. It was near midnight, and the flow of people was thick. I realized that we had never been to the café this late in the evening.

With all the booths filled, we made our way to a table. I looked around the bustling café and saw for myself what I had only wondered might happen in history.

They were here: the men who would kill tens of millions of innocent human beings were all in the same space at the same time. They were in front of me.

Louise, Putzi, Doc, and I adjusted our napkins and silverware. Gunther, who was working late today, arrived sans Frieda and her lost front tooth. It was far too late—and far too evil an environment—for little girls.

Trotsky was to our right, seated at a table next to Lenin, speaking Russian. Approaching them was the bedraggled young Georgian, Stalin, with a heavy, rough suitcase in tow. They shook hands, and Stalin took his seat at their table.

Teenaged Tito was behind them, unaware of this moment in time.

Doc nudged me as we both saw the moment unfolding. He whispered, "Stalin is meeting Lenin for the very first time, right before our eyes."

Putzi and Louise were concluding their conversation and getting settled at the table, looking at us to fill in the meaning of our whispering.

Gunther took our order and removed himself to the kitchen. I saw him return and move toward the table of future communist patriarchs. Two tables away from us on the opposite side was young Adolf Hitler, dressed just "in his heavy boots, dark suit and leather waistcoat and odd little moustache," as Putzi had written in his book. We pointed him out to Putzi.

"He looks like a suburban hairdresser on his day off," Putzi said. Louise laughed. Doc and I had already read these words in Putzi's book. Apparently, so had the clever and erudite Putzi. Maybe a little too clever. Oh, and stealing his own quotes. Hmmm.

Then it happened.

As Gunther approached their table, Leon Trotsky motioned him away with the rude wave of his hand, as if dismissing a lesser person. Gunther stood his ground, demanding through his actions that something should occur. I could not hear their words. But I saw Trotsky stand, puff out his chest toward Gunther, and then slap the waiter across the face. I'd never seen anything like this at any restaurant in any spacetime dimension—which seemed strange as I even thought about it.

Gunther's reaction brought my thinking back to center focus. He recovered, rubbed his cheek, and took a step back. Then he suddenly snapped his fingers at his fellow waiters, and in an instant, four burly Austrian waiters were upon the belligerent guest. They began the process of ejecting young comrade Trotsky. At that moment, his table mates, Lenin and Stalin, stood and objected to the strong reactions by the café staff and began to disparage the waiters. The tensions grew, and the shoving followed. The waiters' clear objective was ejection.

In what seemed like slow motion, I saw Stalin remove a pistol from his loose clothing and point it at Gunther, screaming something in German with a heavy Russian accent. Gunther slapped the barrel of the weapon away from his face, and a round was discharged, striking a nearby customer in the temple, killing him instantly. It was young Josip Tito, a worker at the local car plant. He was dead before he hit the ground.

The café erupted in slow-motion chaos. Stalin fired another round as Gunther pushed backward, the round this time striking Lenin in the left leg, clearly severing an artery, witnessed by the immediate eruption of blood everywhere. The father of communism in Russia fell to the floor in Austria, life flowing out of him. Trotsky lunged for Stalin's pistol, and the crazed Georgian peasant released another round into the chest of the founder and publisher of Pravda, killing Trotsky instantly.

Additional rounds were discharged as customers fell to the floor, some to hide, some because they were injured.

As if to end this nightmare by sacrifice, Gunther hurled himself at Stalin, and the final round was released.

Doc, Putzi, Louise, and I were huddled in a human mass behind our upturned table as silence descended on Café Central.

Slowly, moans interrupted the gun-powdered silence, and we could hear Gunther and another waiter as they subdued Joseph Stalin, the accidental killer of his own cause.

Ensuring that it was safe to stand and exit, many patrons left. Some kindhearted ones surveyed the bloody scene to see if they could help the innocent victims still struggling for life.

We joined the second group.

A beautiful Viennese woman in her twenties had been shot in the side, but the bullet appeared to be somewhat superficial. Louise helped her. Doc helped a middle-aged man with a beard who was knocked over by a flying table as people scrambled for safety when the bullets began. The middle-aged man's face seemed vaguely familiar. His gratitude for being found alive was sincere.

I looked behind me and saw two dead individuals. One was a young man in his twenties, who it turned out was a waiter on his night off who had come in to see a work friend. The other man was facedown, dressed in a leather waistcoat with heavy boots on. I turned him over onto his back, just to ensure he was not alive. His eyes held the death stare common to all humankind at the conclusion of their lives.

His odd little moustache set him apart from all who had died that day.

As police descended on the bullet-ridden café, the waiters began spoiling their brilliantly white napkins and towels by sopping up the large puddles of blood from the floor. Six rounds from a peasant's pistol opened the floodgates of crimson red.

Putzi, Doc, Louise, and I remained in the café to see how we could help the waitstaff, Gunther in particular.

The middle-aged man steadied himself as he rose to his feet from the chair where Doc had placed him. "I thank you for your help tonight." Doc acknowledged his comment.

The man with the nicely trimmed beard asked, "What is your name?"

"I'm Dr. Russell Gersema from America."

"A doctor? So am I. My practice is just around the corner and upstairs. I come here often at night for peace and solitude; it is a good place to think. Tonight was no exception—yet it ended up being the complete exception." Doc and he smiled and then shook hands as the kind man began to leave.

Gunther noticed that the man's hat was still lying on the floor, so he scooped it up and called out, "Dr. Freud, your hat. You mustn't forget your hat."

Doc and I looked at each other as the hat was returned. Doc slowly turned to Louise. Together they looked at Putzi.

"Herr Hitler is dead. Our need to enter into the hard things of your autobiography no longer applies," Doc said. Louise held him around the waist, nodding. Their love for each other was deeply apparent.

"Ja, you are correct, Herr Doctor. And yet …"

We could see that Putzi's mind was on something very deep and disturbing. He continued, "And yet the need to deal with— what was his name?"

"Ernst Röhm."

"Ja, Ernst Röhm! The need to deal with him is clear. We cannot let him attack Washington, DC, London, and Paris to kill the leaders. We cannot let him kill all the Jews. He must be stopped. And along with that, we only have—*according to Isaac Newton*—till 2060 to end this madness."

I couldn't resist. "Why, Putzi, you sound like one of history's fearless men, looking to the future—to trust in what we cannot see."

He looked at me, no longer with the sneer of an aristocrat from Austria but instead with the kind eyes of a redeemed man who had just escaped death.

"Author, all the moments in our lives are summed up by that statement."

Directly outside Café Central, I could see a lone figure with powerful, piercing eyes staring at me.

I had seen his face somewhere before, but where? *The security camera, the photograph!*

I slowly walked out of the café and toward him to see what would happen.

His face was contorted; he opened his mouth and spoke to me. His words were vicious.

"This changes nothing," he said to me. "Hitler, Stalin, Trotsky, and the rest of them are just like any I choose to use or to allow to die. They're nothing to me, and whatever you do will not change the ultimate impact I have on history."

Lafayette Backus was looking directly into my eyes.

I returned his glare and then said, clearly and with no emotion, "You are a liar and a deceiver, a murderer and a thief. And I will see you dead."

He cackled. "*You* will die one day. However, I will just postpone it for myself, moving forward and backward through the river of time, through the skies and from the planets. You will not stop me."

Pointing back toward the café, as my friends exited and were coming toward me, he added, "I'll lay waste to *all* their souls and especially to *your* soul." His words were brutal, his sneer demonic. I was about six feet from him.

He did not scare me. It was now my time to attack.

Arms outstretched, I rushed at him just as he placed his hand on a piece of paper and stepped onto a telluric current. In an instant, he was gone.

Epilogue

We returned to Doc's flat, exhausted and deeply shaken. The deaths at the café along with the threats by Lafayette Backus left us all undone.

To soothe emotions, Dr. Russell Gersema walked over to the shelf with the Edison record player on it. He searched his scattered albums and then put on a Beatles song—an instrumental piece. He next moved to the wet bar and began getting Cokes for us.

Putzi, Louise, and I plopped onto any available plush sofa or chair, trying to process what we had just experienced at Café Central.

The future-ancient Edison phonograph began to turn; its scratchy volume increased. A young Liverpool man's voice came on, introducing the tune. "Louise, Please Cry for a Shadow." It was Stu Sutcliff.

Louise, Doc, and I stopped and smiled. The music was beautiful. The memory even more so.

Next to me, lying on the table, was volume 2 of U. S. Grant's memoirs. I gently shook my head in a wondering sort of way as I glanced at it.

That book began it all, I thought. And then for no apparent reason, I opened it to the cover page.

Under Orrin Backus's old signature was a recently written comment for me.

To Will Clark, our amazing Author.
I trusted in what I could not see because of you.
Now, go finish the job before 2060 happens.
Your friend,
Captain Orrin Backus

Works Consulted

Arbuckle, Alex. "The Tragic Life of Stuart Sutcliffe, the 'fifth Beatle.'" Mashable. October 22, 2015. https://mashable. com/2015/10/22/beatles-stuart-sutcliffe/#7v5vYUwTFEqP.

"Beer Hall Putsch." Wikipedia. https://en.wikipedia.org/wiki/ Beer_Hall_Putsch.

Bellis, Mary. "Meet the Banjo-Playing Engineer Who Invented Scotch Tape." ThoughtCo. https://www.thoughtco.com/ history-of-scotch-tape-1992403.

Best, Pete, and Patrick Doncaster. *Beatle!: The Pete Best Story.* London: Plexus, 2001.

"Biography of Orrin Backus." Access Genealogy. September 14, 2011. https://www.accessgenealogy.com/california/biography-of-orrin-backus.htm.

Blakemore, Erin. "The Rules About How to Address the U.S. Flag Came About Because No One Wanted to Look Like a Nazi." Smithsonian.com. August 12, 2016. https://www. smithsonianmag.com/smart-news/rules-about-how-to-address-us-flag-came-about-because-no-one-wanted-to-look-like-a-nazi-180960100/.

Britannica, The Editors of Encyclopaedia. "Hank Morgan." Encyclopædia Britannica. February 11, 2011. https://www. britannica.com/topic/Hank-Morgan.

Campbell, Bruce. *The SA Generals and the Rise of Nazism.* Lexington: University Press of Kentucky, 2015.

Churchill, Winston. *The Gathering Storm: The Second World War.* London: Penguin Books.

"Civil War Sharpshooters: Col. Hiram Berdan's Creation." Owlcation. https://owlcation.com/humanities/ Civil-War-Sharpshooters-Col-Hiram-Berdans-Creation.

"Coke's Cocaine Problem and Coca-Cola Capitalism." *OUPblog,* January 15, 2015. https://blog.oup.com/2014/03/ coke-cocaine-coca-cola-capitalism-business-strategy/.

Courtney, Steve. "A New Theory On How Samuel L. Clemens Got The Name Mark Twain." Courant.com. January 27, 2014. http://www.courant.com/courant-250/moments-in-history/ hc-twain-name-theory-20140126-story.html.

"CV Sigmund Freud." Sigmund Freud: Chronology. https:// www.freud-museum.at/en/sigmund-and-anna-freud/vita-sigmund-freud.html.

Czarina Ong. Monday, March 23, 2015, 12:03 GMT. "Why MercyMe's Dear Younger Me Is One of the Hardest Songs They Ever Had to Write." Christian News on Christian Today. March 23, 2015. https://www.christiantoday.com/article/why-mercymes-dear-younger-me-is-one-of-the-hardest-songs-they-ever-had-to-write/50493.htm.

Deffner, Sebastian. "Static Electricity's Tiny Sparks." The Conversation. June 19, 2018. http://theconversation.com/ static-electricitys-tiny-sparks-70637.

"Department of Archaeology." Fluorometer—Biology, the University of York. https://www.york.ac.uk/archaeology/staff/ research-staff/fiddyment/.

Downes, Lawrence. "Mark Twain's Hawaii." *New York Times,* May 14, 2006. https://www.nytimes.com/2006/05/14/ travel/14twain.html.

Dry, Sarah. *The Newton Papers: The Strange and True Odyssey of Isaac Newton's Manuscripts.* Oxford: Oxford University Press, 2014.

"E=mc2." *American Journal of Human Genetics*; (United States). https://www.osti.gov/accomplishments/nuggets/einstein/ speedoflight.html.

Einstein, Albert. "Einstein on Newton." PBS. November 15, 2005. http://www.pbs.org/wgbh/nova/physics/einstein-on-newton.html.

Elmore, Bartow Jerome. "Coca-Cola Has Always Had a Connection to the Cocaine Business." *Huffington Post*, September 2, 2016. https://www.huffingtonpost.com/entry/ coca-cola-has-always-had-a-connection-to-the-cocaine_us_ 57c8757ae4b07addc4119330.

"Emigrants to a New World Gallery." National Museums Liverpool. http://www.liverpoolmuseums.org.uk/maritime/ visit/floor-plan/emigration/.

"Ernst Röhm." Claus Von Stauffenberg. http://www. jewishvirtuallibrary.org/ernst-r-ouml-hm.

"Family Tree of Katharine Whetten Sedgwick." Geneanet. https://gw.geneanet.org/frebault?lang=en&pz=henri&nz= frebault&ocz=0&p=katharine whetten&n=sedgwick.

Frampton, Peter. Personal conversation and interview in Boise, Idaho. August 2018.

Gold, Charles H. *"Hatching Ruin," Or, Mark Twain's Road to Bankruptcy*. Columbia: University of Missouri Press, 2003.

"Gone—Pete Best Band." SongLyrics.com. http://www. songlyrics.com/pete-best-band/gone-lyrics/.

Gottsman, Diane. "TIPS: To Insure Prompt Service (and Other Useful Acronyms)." Diane Gottsman | Etiquette Expert, Modern Manners & Leader in Business Etiquette. March 15, 2016. https://dianegottsman.com/2014/04/16/ tips-to-insure-prompt-service-and-other-useful-acronyms/.

Grant, Ulysses S. *Personal Memoirs of U. S. Grant*, vol. 1 and vol. 2. 1885.

Greene, Brian. *The Elegant Universe*. Boston: NOVA, 2003.

Greene, Brian. "Making Sense of String Theory." April 23, 2008. http://www.briangreene.org/portfolio/making-sense-of-string-theory/.

Greene, Brian (Staff). Correspondence with staff 2018 and 2019.

"Two Computer Scientists Who Disagreed on Everything Found Google." Haaretz.com. April 10, 2018. https://www.haaretz.com/jewish/2-computer-scientists-found-google-1.5394903.

Hanfstaengl, Ernst. *Hitler: The Missing Years*. New York: Arcade Publishers, 1994.

Hays, Jeffrey. "World War II and the Soviet Union." Facts and Details. http://factsanddetails.com/russia/History/sub9_1e/entry-4971.html.

Hernandez, Daniel. "A New Theory on 'Mark Twain.'" Los Angeles Review of Books. https://lareviewofbooks.org/article/a-new-theory-on-mark-twain#!

Hernandez, Daniel. "Mark Twain Was a Brand." Salon. September 28, 2013. https://www.salon.com/2013/09/28/mark_twain_cunningly_created_his_brand_partner/.

"Historical Oddities: 1913, When Seven Men Who Shaped History All Lived in Vienna." The Time Stream. October 03, 2013. https://thetimestream.wordpress.com/2013/10/03/historical-oddities-1913-when-seven-men-who-shaped-history-all-lived-in-vienna/.

"History." Harvard University. https://www.harvard.edu/about-harvard/harvard-glance/history.

History.com Staff. "Mark Twain." History.com. 2010. https://www.history.com/topics/mark-twain.

"Hitler Sketches That Failed to Secure His Place at Art Academy to Be Auctioned." *Telegraph*. March 24, 2010. https://www.telegraph.co.uk/culture/art/art-news/7511134/Hitler-sketches-that-failed-to-secure-his-place-at-art-academy-to-be-auctioned.html.

"Hitler's Harvard Man: Ernst Hanfstaengl." HistoryNet. May 11, 2017. http://www.historynet.com/hitlers-harvard-man-ernst-hanfstaengl.htm.

Hitler, Adolf. *Mein Kampf.* Franz Eher Nachfolger, 1925.

Hitler, Adolf, Gerhard L. Weinberg, and Krista Smith. *Hitlers Second Book: The Unpublished Sequel to Mein Kampf.* New York: Enigma Books, 2006.

"Hitler: The Missing Years / Ernst ('Putzi') Hanfstaengl. - Version Details." Trove. https://trove.nla.gov.au/work/10995740?selectedversion=NBD10518411.

Hummel, Charles E. "The Faith Behind the Famous: Isaac Newton." Christian History | Learn the History of Christianity & the Church. https://www.christianitytoday.com/history/issues/issue-30/faith-behind-famous-isaac-newton.html.

Josephy, Alvin M. "Giants in the Earth." *New York Times.* https://archive.nytimes.com/www.nytimes.com/books/97/03/02/bsp/undaunted.html.

"Kaiserkeller." Wikipedia. June 26, 2018. https://en.wikipedia.org/wiki/Kaiserkeller.

King, Gilbert. "War and Peace of Mind for Ulysses S. Grant." Smithsonian.com. January 16, 2013. https://www.smithsonianmag.com/history/war-and-peace-of-mind-for-ulysses-s-grant-1882227/.

King, Stephen. *On Writing.* New York, NY: Simon & Schuster, 2000.

King, Chris. "The Forgotten Home Team in Hartford." *New York Times*, April 13, 2003. https://www.nytimes.com/2003/04/13/nyregion/the-forgotten-home-team-in-hartford.html.

Landers, Chris. "Mark Twain Once Had His Umbrella Stolen at a Baseball Game." MLB.com. https://www.mlb.com/cut4/mark-twain-once-had-his-umbrella-stolen-at-a-baseball-game/c-230539632.

"Leon Trotsky." Biography.com. April 28, 2017. https://www.biography.com/people/leon-trotsky-9510793.

"Mark Twain." Depression-era Soup Kitchens. http://www.u-s-history.com/pages/h3702.html.

"Mark Twain." Peanuts—Wikiquote. https://en.wikiquote.org/
wiki/Mark_Twain.

"Mark Twain Has Filed Bankruptcy!" RSS.
https://considerchapter13.org/2012/12/08/
mark-twain-has-filed-bankruptcy/.

"Max Abraham." Clavius Biography. http://www-groups.dcs.st-
and.ac.uk/history/Biographies/Abraham_Max.html.

Midgley, Dominic. "Astrid Kirchherr: The Woman Who
Gave The Beatles Their Style." Express.co.uk. December
03, 2014. https://www.express.co.uk/life-style/style/543217/
Astrid-Kirchherr-woman-gave-The-Beatles-their-style.

Mills, Billy. "The Old Straight Track by Alfred Watkins—
Walking through the past." *Guardian*, August 20, 2015. https://
www.theguardian.com/books/booksblog/2015/aug/20/the-
old-straight-track-by-alfred-watkins-walking-through-the-past.

"Mona Best." Wikipedia. https://en.wikipedia.org/wiki/Mona_
Best.

Nelson, Raelyn. Email correspondence with Willie Nelson's
website, August 2018 and May 2019.

Nixon, Richard M. *Six Crises*. London: W.H. Allen, 1962.

"Not the Best Idea." Business Lessons from Rock. February 11,
2017. http://businesslessonsfromrock.com/notes/2017/02/
not-the-best-idea/.

"Paul McCartney: The Beatles' Other Drummer." *DRUM!*
magazine, August 30, 2016. http://drummagazine.com/
paul-mccartney-the-beatles-other-drummer/.

"PETE BEST." Home | Official Pete Best. http://www.petebest.
com/casbah-coffee-club.aspx.

Phoenix, J., Esquire. "Sedgwick's Spurs." Past in Review. https://
www.westpointaog.org/document.doc?id=4962.

Rasmussen, R. Kent, *Critical Companion to Mark Twain: A Literary
Reference to His Life and Work*. New York: Facts on File, 2007.

"Record Speed Became 33 1/3 In A Roundabout Way."
Tribunedigital-chicagotribune. June 15, 1986. http://articles.

chicagotribune.com/1986-06-15/features/8602120863_1_
discs-speeds-long-playing-record.

"Re: Stu's Injury Caused by John?" *Playboy* interview: John
Lennon and Yoko Ono. http://www.recmusicbeatles.com/
public/files/bbs/stu.html.

"Release of Stuart Sutcliffe's Historical Recording of
'Love Me Tender.'" Escouter News. http://myemail.
constantcontact.com/Release-of-Stuart-Sutcliffe-
s-Historical-Recording-of--Love-Me-Tender-.
html?soid=1108302654045&aid=WqMl-HIAmEw.

"Roman Salute." Wikipedia. https://en.wikipedia.org/wiki/
Roman_salute.

Röhm, Ernst, Eleanor Hancock, and Geoffrey Brooks. *The
Memoirs of Ernst Röhm*. Barnsley: Frontline Books, 2012.

Shirer, William Lawrence. *The Rise and Fall of the Third Reich: A
History of Nazi Germany*. London: Arrow, 1998.

Spasowski, Romuald. *The Liberation of One*. San Diego: Harcourt
Brace Jovanovich, 1987.

"Steyr M1912." Literary Merit. https://ipfs.io/ipfs/
QmXoypizjW3WknFiJnKLwHCnL72vedxjQk
DDPlmXWo6uco/wiki/Steyr_M1912.html.

Stone, Sarah, and Sarah Stone—TodayIFoundOut.com. "How
the Tea Bag Was Invented." Gizmodo. April 27, 2015. https://
gizmodo.com/how-the-tea-bag-was-invented-1700351584.

Sutcliffe, Pauline and Diane. Email correspondence, June and
October 2018, January 2019.

Taylor, James. "Secret O' Life." Recorded 1977.

"Telluric Current." Wikipedia. https://en.wikipedia.org/wiki/
Telluric_current.

"The American Express Card (October 1, 1958)." About
HistoryofInformation.com. http://www.historyofinformation.
com/expanded.php?id=2051.

"The Beatle Cocktail." Classic Cocktails and Bar Equipment
UK. https://www.cocktail.uk.com/cocktails/the-beatle.

"The Beatles—The Best Year—The Complete Recordings of Pete Best and the Beatles—June 1961 to June 1962." Discogs. https://www.discogs.com/The-Beatles-The-Best-Year-The-Complete-Recordings-Of-Pete-Best-And-The-Beatles-June-1961-To-June-196/release/4194836.

"The Beatles on the *Ed Sullivan Show*." *Ed Sullivan Show*. http://www.edsullivan.com/the-beatles-on-the-ed-sullivan-show-on-february-9-1964/.

"The Beatles' First Performance in Hamburg." The Beatles Bible. March 23, 2018. https://www.beatlesbible.com/1960/08/17/live-indra-club-hamburg/.

"The Death of General John Sedgwick." Soldiers Pay in the American Civil War. http://www.civilwarhome.com/sedgwickdeath.htm.

"The Death of John Sedgwick." American Battlefield Trust. May 09, 2018. https://www.battlefields.org/learn/articles/death-john-sedgwick.

The Franz Hanfstaengl Publishing Company. http://www.blanc-kunstverlag.de/en/the-franz-hanfstaengl-publishing-company.

"The History of 'Mate.'" *Oxford Australia Blog*. December 11, 2017. https://blog.oup.com.au/2016/01/the-history-of-mate/.

The Torah: The Five Books of Moses.

Thill, Scott. "June 21, 1948: Columbia's Microgroove LP Makes Albums Sound Good." Wired. January 14, 2018. https://www.wired.com/2010/06/0621first-lp-released/.

"Timeline." Timeline and History // Resources T. http://bancroft.berkeley.edu/Exhibits/mtatplay/timeline/timeline.html.

Twain, Mark, and William M. Gibson. *Mark Twain's Mysterious Stranger Manuscripts*. Berkeley and Los Angeles: University of California Press, 1969.

Twain, Mark. "Twain's Conversations with Satan." The Daily Beast. April 26, 2009. https://www.thedailybeast.com/twains-conversations-with-satan.

Twain, Mark, Benjamin Griffin, Harriet Elinor Smith, Victor Fischer, and Michael B. Frank. *Autobiography of Mark Twain: Complete and Authoritative Edition*. Berkeley, CA: University of California Press, 2013.

"Twain Hawaii Letter: March 1866." Twain Library. http://twain.lib.virginia.edu/roughingit/mthawlet1.html.

"Twain in Vienna." The Vienna Review. https://www.viennareview.net/news/austria/twain-in-vienna.

"Twain's Farewell to Vienna." Anna Amalie Tutein—Blind Tom's Teacher. http://www.twainquotes.com/18990611.html.

"UK Tea & Infusions Association—The History of the Tea Bag." UK Tea & Infusions Association—Tea—A Brief History of the Nation's Favourite Beverage. https://www.tea.co.uk/the-history-of-the-tea-bag.

"Vladimir Lenin." Biography.com. April 28, 2017. https://www.biography.com/people/vladimir-lenin-9379007.

Walker, Andy. "1913: When Hitler, Trotsky, Tito, Freud and Stalin All Lived in the Same Place." BBC News. April 18, 2013. https://www.bbc.com/news/magazine-21859771.

Wall, Maryjean. "The Horse That Birthed the Beatles." *Wall Street Journal*, May 24, 2013. https://www.wsj.com/articles/SB10001424127887323744604578474872518503546.

Walsh, John. "Being Ernest: John Walsh Unravels the Mystery behind Hemingway's." *Independent*, October 23, 2011. https://www.independent.co.uk/news/people/profiles/being-ernest-john-walsh-unravels-the-mystery-behind-hemingways-suicide-2294619.html.

Watkins, Alfred. *The Old Straight Track: Its Mounds, Beacons, Moats, Sites, and Mark Stones*. Glastonbury: Lost Library, 2013.

Weslo, Joey. "Theoretical Physicist Brian Greene Proposes String Theory as the Theory of Everything." *Courier*, April 4, 2018. https://codcourier.org/8400/news/theoretical-physicist-brian-greene-proposes-string-theory-as-the-theory-of-everything/.

"Who Killed Uncle John (and John Reynolds)?" *TOCWOC—A Civil War Blog*, December 7, 2008. http://www.brettschulte.net/CWBlog/2008/12/06/who-killed-uncle-john-and-john-reynolds/.

"Wien." Home. http://www.hitlerpages.com/pagina26a.html.

Zacks, Richard. "How Mark Twain Lost a Fortune in 19th-Century Start-Up Fails." *Time*, April 19, 2016. http://time.com/4297572/mark-twain-bad-business/.

Zorich, Zach. "The Hidden Stories of the York Gospel." *Archaeology* magazine. https://www.archaeology.org/issues/275-1711/from-the-trenches/6014-trenches-england-york-gospel-dna.

Coming soon: Volume II of To Trust In What We Cannot See

What if history had just a few slight changes that stopped assassinations and death?
What would stay the same and what would change drastically?
Who would lead?

Here's a taste of what's next in Volume II:

Hannibal Hamlin, President of the United Sates after President Abraham Lincoln was impeached by the US House of Representatives and found guilty by the US Senate in 1863.

Henry Wallace, President of the United States after President Franklin D. Roosevelt died in 1944, just a few months earlier in history.

John Hay, President of the United States, former Secretary of State and former Private Secretary to former President Abraham Lincoln. He tried to carry on Lincoln's legacy but failed.

Two Presidents of the United States: President Robert F. Kennedy and President Michael King, Jr. Accidents and the deaths of others kept them alive to lead.

President of the United States, Alben Barkley, friend to young Senator John F. Kennedy.

General G. Armstrong Custer, President of the United States, enemy of U. S. Grant. He was never sent to the Little Big Horn; he was sent into history in a different way.

American children during the 1930s and '40s. Hitler was gone but German Leader Ernst Röhm was not.

President John F. Kennedy survived Oswald.

Printed in the United States
by Baker & Taylor Publisher Services